C000260226

Time

Wisdom

& Koalas

Time

Wisdom

&

Koalas

David Miller

chax 2023

Time, Wisdom and Koalas
ISBN 978-1-946104-41-0
Copyright ©2023 by David Miller

Library of Congress Control Number: 2023932126

Trade Paperback Edition published by
Chax Press
1517 N Wilmot Rd no. 264
Tucson, AZ 85712
USA

Chax acknowledges the support of interns and assistants who contribute
to the books we publish, including David Weiss, Ben Leitner, and Cynthia
Miller.

This book is also supported by private donors. We are thankful to all of our
contributors and members. Please see http://chax.org for more information,
and please consider supporting our work.

Cover art: *'Dodo's'* (ink painting), copyright © David Miller, 2023
Frontispiece: Koala drawing by David Miller, copyright © David Miller, 2023

in memory of Dodo, with love

contents

Beyond the Mirror of the Fatal Shore

Part One

1.

"Those dark-skinned people believe that we're wise! And so we are!" Norm said to himself.

He meant the Aborigines of his homeland, who hunted his kind and yet held them in respect.

So what if he and his fellow koalas slept for most of the day and spent much of their waking time eating eucalyptus leaves? They still had a richly reflective life.

But what had made him think back to what the Aborigines said?

He was, you might say, *a stranger in a strange land*: twice over, as it happened. He had also been on the run; and, for all he knew, still was.

And badly in need of alternatives.

2.

The facts are as follows:

From an early age, Norm had been given to wandering, far more and far further than most koalas.

And on those wanderings he made many friends, some of whom had unusual things to share with him. For example, one learned old koala taught him the basics of the English language, while others helped him to become proficient in Aboriginal tongues.

However, knowledge was not wisdom as such, not as far as Norm was concerned. Wisdom came from immersing yourself in nature and in the dream life; it came from contemplation and deep understanding; and it also came from setting your heart at ease.

Not that there weren't things other koalas could share with you that led to wisdom. Norm would never deny that. Indeed, that period of his life, he often thought, could be chiefly characterised by his encounters with Extraordinary Koalas.

The most important of these encounters occurred in a remote and barely accessible place little known to either people or koalas. Norm had heard rumours of it and was determined to find it.

Find it he did, after much searching and difficult travelling. A colony of koalas had formed itself there, or perhaps a school or academy might be a better term. They were wise beyond anything Norm had encountered before.

These koalas taught but also listened and were taught in turn. Everything was shared. And nothing was simply taken for granted, but questioned and interpreted anew.

Norm stayed for many months. But eventually he decided to leave. He wanted a home and a community of his own, where he could impart his wisdom and improve the lives of ordinary koalas.

So off he set.

He found the place and the denizens he desired in the bush lands of New

South Wales. He became the Koala Elder of many in the area. He taught them to live peacefully together and to be faithful to their companions, as well as divers other things... including minor skills such as understanding and speaking English. More than anything else, he taught devotion and service to the Great Spirit Koala, the source of all good things. The community thrived.

Then the attack occurred. It was sudden, unexpected, brutal. White men knocked the koalas from their trees into nets and pursued them if they managed to evade the nets and run. Blows, kicks, curses. Koalas bellowed and screamed; joeys cried.

Norm was amongst those who were taken into captivity and transported from their native land, undergoing a long and cruel voyage by sea. Sufferings were great. Many died.

Herne Bay in England was their destination. There a compound had been built for the captives. Why? Because a crazy and charismatic businessman persuaded backers to set it up, the object being to use koalas as slave labour for the commercial production of eucalyptus oil.

If Botany Bay and other destinations in Australia had been the "fatal shore" for convicts sent from England, so Herne Bay became the mirror of the fatal shore for these poor marsupials.

The enterprise didn't work, of course. It was simply impracticable; but it took a little while for the backers to realise this. When they did, they decided to sell the captive animals for medical experimentation.

Before this could happen, there was a revolt. A koala named David scaled the wire fence, with the help of Norm and the others, and made his escape.

He found his way to a river, which turned out to be the River of Time, and attempted to swim across it. He was picked up by some people in a row boat... and found himself not in the early 1800s anymore, but in the 1930s.

All this is well known, of course: the captivity narrative, and David's escape and subsequent history; hence the bare recital.

The rest of Norman's story is scarcely known at all.

3.

After David's escape, Norm knew that security would be increased in the compound, and that he and the others needed to act quickly.

So while almost all the guards were still trying to track David down, Norm led a concerted rush upon the fence and upon the one remaining human in the compound. The koalas knew their lives were at stake; Norm had already told them to put aside their belief in peacefulness for the time being, after there'd been talk amongst the guards of ripping out their claws and teeth. Now he called for an attack *en masse*. Scratching with their powerful claws, biting, even pissing – for koala urine is peculiarly strong due to their exclusive diet of eucalyptus leaves – the koalas overwhelmed the guard and set out for freedom.

Norm advised that they all go separate ways, to increase their chances. He would never see any of his comrades again, or know of their fate. Through his dreams, though, he eventually had intimations, according to which some were killed; some starved; some simply disappeared.

Norm travelled for several days, ever fearful he was being pursued and would be caught. He stopped to sleep only when he really had to – though as koalas sleep most of the day, that was actually fairly often. Even so, he was exhausted when he found himself on the banks of a river. He decided to cross it, and dove in.

4.

Two men were rowing on the river. One was tall and lanky, with dark hair and glasses; the other was tall and plump and had ginger hair, and wore a self-possessed look – one might possibly say he appeared arrogant. You wouldn't have known quite how tall they were if you observed them from where Norm was, however.

"What's that dark shape, Aldous?" one of them said. "It seems to be swimming towards us."

"I can't see anything, Humbert, old boy."

"Yes! Look – I think it's one of those koala thingies."

"Nonsense. Anyway, I still can't see anything."

"I keep telling you: you need better glasses, Aldous."

"Ah! Now I see the thingy."

"That's because it's right alongside. Help me pull it on board: I think it's in trouble."

Norm offered no resistance. He felt extremely tired and feeble, and he knew he couldn't swim for any longer. Koalas are not used to swimming. He could probably have still given them a scratch or two, but he didn't even try. It was a matter of trusting these humans – difficult for a koala to do – or drown.

Norm collapsed into the boat.

"What are we going to do with him?" Humbert asked. "I know it was my idea to bring him on board. But we don't want to be late for the conference!"

"Why, we'll bring him along, of course."

"But it's a private conference, for the invited – not the general public. It's even supposed to be somewhat secret, in fact."

"I don't think anyone's going to mind, old man – after all, he's a small animal, not a person. And I hardly think the little chap will tell anyone."

"Ah, you're right of course, Aldous. Why not bring him along, indeed."

"But look here, Humbert, old boy, why was *I* invited? I don't believe all this stuff you believe, nor what I guess will be on offer where we're going."

"Let's face it, Aldous: your humorous, cynical novels about disillusioned characters have brought you success, granted. But will they be remembered? I'm afraid I really doubt it, old chap. Whereas a spiritual Adept like me – Humbert J Brockenhurst – my name will be remembered forever."

"That doesn't answer my question, Humbert. And besides, I don't think that's entirely accurate about my novels."

"Perhaps not. Indeed, I think the organisers have seen something in your writing, Aldous, which could be *developed*. I believe I can almost see it myself. In point of fact, I dare say I've glimpsed spiritual potential in you ever since we were at Eton together."

"I suppose that's gratifying," Aldous sighed.

5.

The koala named David had landed in the 1930s when he emerged from the River of Time: for that was indeed what the river was, as I've said. It was safe to cross it by boat, but not to swim in it. Those who did found themselves in different parts of history, and usually went mad – or at least were believed to be so when they tried to tell their strange tales. The River retained a strange reputation that made few chance to swim in it, though past disappearances assumed the form of folklore, and the odd contemporary occurrence tended to be explained away.

Norm had arrived in the 1920s. For a koala, you might think that finding yourself in the 1920s – or '30s for that matter – wouldn't make all that much difference to where you started, in Norm's case in the early 1800s; especially when it's a foreign land anyway.

The most important things, at least to begin with, are food and safety.

But for an especially intelligent koala like Norm, everything seemed quite disorienting. He did not go mad, however. He wisely struggled to adjust himself to the fact that things simply didn't look the same and quite likely weren't. It would be some time before he guessed the truth of what had happened to him. And even then he didn't become insane.

He let Aldous carry him when the two men had landed at their destination and began walking towards a property with a group of large buildings. He was too exhausted to do much else, and he had begun to trust this pair.

"Luck's on your side, little fellow," said Humbert, "I know for a fact that there are a couple of eucalyptus trees in the grounds – over that way, where I'm pointing."

Norm didn't need to be told twice. He revived at the magical sound of the word "eucalyptus". As weak as he was, he climbed down and managed to scamper off – after a fashion – in the direction of the gum trees.

"By George," said Humbert. "You'd think the furry rascal understood me!"

When Norm found Aldous and Humbert again, they were about to enter one of the halls to attend a talk. Norm went along with them.

He found himself an object – or should I say subject – of attention at this and the other gatherings he went to with Aldous and Humbert. Women especially found him fascinating. "Gorgeous!" "Oh, how cute!" "He's a darling!"

He took it all in his stride, being a wise koala.

Norm noticed someone digging a large ditch in the grounds, quite close to one of the halls. The digger was dressed too well to be a gardener or manual labourer and didn't look especially happy about what he was doing; also, there was no obvious reason for the ditch, at least as far as Norm could discern. A formidable-looking man with a completely bald head and a large, fierce moustache came and berated the digger from time to time. Norm recognised the formidable man as one of the speakers – probably the main speaker, given the deference others gave him. The whole thing seemed crazy; but after all, they were human beings: what could you expect?

The talks were long and frequent. Norm slept through many of them, or in some cases through parts of them. But he did pick up on quite a good deal, just the same.

Most of the speakers had come from London or from Paris and Fontainebleau, along with the odd visitor from America.

There was much talk of the Work and much talk of the System. It all sounded confused, and sometimes even silly. These people seemed to believe that most humans were asleep when they thought they were awake, and had to really wake up. "*If only!*" Norm thought. Sleep's wonderful – it rests and revives you, and you go on strange journeys, some of which are definitely spirit journeys. In sleep, koalas look even more beautiful than when they're awake. Koalas sleep for as long as possible, with good reason and to wonderful effect! Waking time is sustained by sleep and, through spirit dreams, given meaning by it. If humans were really asleep all the time, good luck to them! But it would scarcely seem true. As for this business about "the Work" – it sounded so terribly... *busy.* When would there be time to contemplate? Koalas were good at contemplation. Norm was *extremely* good at it.

"Yes, all right," said Norm to himself, "I'm only a little koala, but at the same time, *I'm wise.* Perhaps I can help these people become less confused. And in turn, perhaps they'll help me with my predicament!"

6.

Humbert was somewhat impressed and also challenged by what he'd heard, and unsure about where it left him as a Theosophical Adept; whereas Aldous was non-committal.

"I wish Krishna had been here to debate with them!" exclaimed Humbert. "Now *that* would have been really interesting."

"*Krishna?* Is he... *blue*? Is he surrounded by milkmaids? Does he play the flute while standing on one leg?"

"No, Aldous, it's simply his name: he's an Indian. But some people do think he's the World Teacher – the Messiah. You should get to know him."

"Perhaps I will."

"I think I can help you," said Norm, walking up to them. "You humans seem very confused. And I'm wise."

"I must be having an out-of-the-body experience!" exclaimed Humbert.

"I don't think *I* am. What is that thing? A precocious infant? A very small dwarf on all fours?"

"It's the koala, Aldous! AND HE'S TALKING!"

"Ah, I did wonder about the fur coat."

"Are you a Mahatma in animal disguise?" Humbert asked Norm. "Ah yes, I think I see a light blue aura surrounding you... no, I think it's actually white! Or are you possibly a being from another planet, disguised as a furry

Antipodean beastie?"

"I'm just a koala," Norm replied.

"You speak English very well," said Aldous.

"I took lessons. I learned a great deal from other koalas, extraordinary koalas, you might say: including the language you speak." He nodded towards them. "But learning wasn't all that I sought. Knowledge is all well and good. Rather, what I wanted was – "

"Wisdom," Aldous volunteered.

"Yes."

"So why don't you begin?" asked Aldous. "Tell us something."

Norm composed himself.

"Koalas love eucalyptus leaves," he began, "and the leaves love their branches and the branches love the tree...."

"I suppose you're going to go on to the air and the sky and the sun and the rain?" interrupted Humbert.

"Well, yes," said Norm, a little puzzled.

"Sentimental blather!" exclaimed Humbert.

"Give him a chance," said Aldous, adjusting his glasses. "By the way, are you sure it really is the koala, and not a very small dwarf in a fur coat?"

"I really am a koala," said Norm, not waiting for Humbert to reply. "Perhaps I should skip a little?"

"Yes, go on," said Humbert irritably. "Let's get it over with."

"If *that's* how you feel….," Norm began, becoming irritated himself.

"Oh, come on, Humbert," said Aldous. "I'd like to hear what the little chap has to say."

"I'm all ears," said Humbert resignedly.

"Koalas feel a kinship, even if somewhat distant, with other beings... especially wombats, possums, wallabies...."

"Can we skip this as well?" asked Humbert.

"That's quite funny, Humbert," said Aldous.

"Oh yes, I see! I hadn't actually meant to make a joke, old boy."

"...antechinus," continued Norm, determined not to be distracted.

"*What?*" exclaimed Humbert.

"It's a sort of marsupial mouse," said Aldous.

"But of course it's with other koalas that we feel most involved, both living koalas and dead, in a never-ending, ever-present, underlying oneness: even if there are many koalas who don't realise this and don't live their lives accordingly. I call it the Communion of Koalas."

"Extraordinary!" said Aldous.

"Balderdash!" countered Humbert.

"Look," said Norm, "I'm trying to impart some wisdom. Something you humans seem short on." He looked directly at Humbert. "By the way, I bet that when you were a boy the other children used to call you Custard Tart."

Humbert turned red in the face. "How on earth did you know that?"

"Just a wild guess."

"But it doesn't even rhyme. It was never funny at all. And I didn't look remotely like one – "

"Calm down," said Aldous, patting Humbert on the arm. "It's long in the past. You can forget it."

Aldous turned to Norm. "I must say, old chap, your English is *really* rather good."

"Thank you. Would you know how to bellow like a koala to other koalas?"

"Well, no. Not really."

"I could always teach you."

"I suppose I was being a little condescending. Sorry."

"Are you sure you're not a member of some Great Furry Lodge, or some other gathering of Adepts and Mahatmas?" interrupted Humbert.

"Let's begin again," said Norm, ignoring him. "The Great Spirit Koala created us, the koalas especially, but also the wombats, antechinus, wallabies, and so on, as well as the sky, the earth, the trees, the rain, the air, because the Great Spirit Koala loves all of us. We are enfolded in the Great Spirit Koala's love, always. That's the basis for the Communion of Koalas. Once we realise this, we gain and become more fully ourselves by entering into the Great Spirit Koala's love and being absorbed in splendour. We don't lose anything, not in the least; we become more fully ourselves by entering into the unity of the Great Spirit Koala's love for us."

"Extraordinary!" said Aldous.

"I'm not even going to say anything," said Humbert.

"Oh, Custard Heart!" said Norm.

"Tart! Tart! Not Heart! And I still don't know why anyone ever called me that!" Humbert was red in the face again and close to tears. "How on earth did you ever know?"

Aldous patted him on the arm. "It's all right, old chap."

"I'm sorry," said Norm. "I didn't realise you'd be so upset."

"But how *did* you know?"

"A wild guess. Really nothing more. But let's continue."

Norm paused. And composed himself.

"Branches and leaves, branches and leaves, branches and leaves," Norm rhapsodised, "with sunlight shining through... grass beneath, and water in pools.

"Branches carry us from one thing to another, and then to another, and so on, and finally to the glory and splendour of the Great Spirit Koala."

He took a breath. "All these things are in a sense branches – and clusters of branches – hills, rivers, wind, water, sunlight, birds, goannas, wombats, other koalas... carrying us all the way to the Great Spirit Koala."

"Aren't you making a bit of a leap there?" Humbert enquired.

"You often have to leap from branch to branch. Branches lead to other branches and to the branches of other trees; they lead to the sky and, following the trunk, to the earth. The way up the trunk is also the way down...."

"Are you quoting Heraclitus?" queried Aldous, looking astonished. "*The way up is the same as the way down?*"

"Who?" asked Norm. "What?"

"Of course the little furry blighter doesn't know Heraclitus," said Humbert.

"A wise man once said that the way up is the way down. His name was Heraclitus," Aldous explained.

"Yes," said Norm. "You climb up a tree the same way you climb down a tree – well, more-or-less."

"Hmm, the little chap's got something there. Ladders, cliffs.... Extraordinary!"

"I don't suppose Heraclitus meant it in a strictly literal sense, Aldous."

"But how *did* he mean it?"

"How should I know? Inscrutable old Greek!"

Norm ignored them and continued:

"A branch from one thing to another, branches clustered together or apart – we go from branch to branch and in the same way from one thing to another. Branches exist everywhere, even if some may not look like a branch. And the branches come from and lead back to the Great Spirit Koala."

He paused.

"But then there are bush fires, and chasms and pits, and the black people's boomerangs... and you white people. Sometimes it all seems impossible. More often than not these things break up our sense of branches and even go against the Great Spirit Koala."

He paused again.

"I certainly wouldn't expect a koala caught in a bush fire to feel anything but terror and suffering. If you burned to death, don't you think you'd suffer? If you were beaten to death, wouldn't you suffer?"

"You don't deny suffering, then?"

"Oh no! Nor evil!"

He paused.

"I think that's enough for this time. I need to sleep."

Norm scampered to one of the eucalyptus trees, climbed it and settled on a branch to sleep. Humbert and Aldous followed him as far as the base of the tree.

"Damn it, he does look beautiful," said Humbert.

"Does he?" Aldous asked. "Well, he'll be asleep for hours and hours. We might as well go to another talk."

7.

"The Great Spirit Koala set things going... everything: that's our understanding," Norm began.

"It's all to do with the Great Spirit Koala allowing something to happen, and that included possibility after possibility, so many possibilities, following on from each other. The possibilities come from the Great Spirit Koala, but they develop on their own."

He paused.

"Some of these possibilities were very much in line with the Great Spirit Koala's own nature: koalas, especially, and the trees and the earth and water and skies and hills. But you humans – I can only think something went wrong after the creation began. I'm only a little koala, I don't know everything..... Though I *am* wise."

"Now look here – " began Humbert.

"Your English really *is* good," said Aldous, cutting Humbert short.

"So you keep telling me."

"Sorry, I forgot myself... I'm being condescending again. So the Great Spirit Koala – can we call it It or He or She, by the way?"

"No."

"All right, the Great Spirit Koala put something in motion, and there were accidents or by-products involved in the process."

Norm cocked his head. "I'm not sure I understand what you're talking about," he said. "I guess there are always... um, regrettable... um, developments of possibilities... everywhere."

"But isn't the Great Spirit Koala incapable of mistakes?"

"Aldous, this is a *koala* we're talking to!" Humbert interrupted.

"Mistakes? Possibilities... or what you call chance."

"Random possibilities," said Aldous.

"It's what you quite likely won't have guessed would happen... the unexpected... what doesn't seem to belong to a pattern. It's where there are all these possibilities, and which will happen and which won't, we can't tell. We can see why some things happen, but these other things defeat us."

He paused, and then continued:

"I couldn't have known that you'd be on that river when I jumped in and when I started to drown, nor could you have known I'd be there. It's what you can't know will happen before it happens. Some of these possibilities will then keep happening, though not always in the same way. You humans happened – forgive me, but that was one of the unfortunate possibilities. And you've kept on happening, but you're not all the same. A small number of you are good, at least by your own standards, and occasionally even by ours. Some of your females, especially. But you two saved my life! You acted in a good way. That's why I've chosen you."

He paused again.

"Your appearing on the river when I was drowning.... That might be *branches!*

But there are other things....I can't see that *they* are."

"They're too haphazard."

"What? I'm sorry?"

"Let's come back to that," suggested Aldous. "Please continue with what you were saying."

"These things, these possibilities, have their own life, almost as koalas do. Their own freedom. They develop by themselves, in relation to other things; but having allowed all this, the Great Spirit Koala doesn't interfere."

"So the Great Spirit Koala allows sets of possibilities," Aldous said, "some of which involve chance, to come into existence. And there is no divine intervention."

"So the Great Spirit Koala is absent from the world?" Humbert chipped in.

"Of course not. There are branches everywhere. We have the Great Spirit Koala's love. We are folded into that love."

"Could things have developed differently?"

"Of course the Great Spirit Koala could have let things happen differently...."

"Then why...?"

"Yes, but this is best for koalas – to develop their freedom of choice."

"Do the same laws operate throughout the universe, without exception? Even for koalas?"

"If you say so. I'm getting tired. I'm going to take a nap."

"You mentioned evil last time..."

"Remind me the next time," said Norm, scampering towards a tree.

"Bugger!" exclaimed Humbert.

"Steady on," said Aldous.

8.

"So the Great Spirit Koala is God?"

"To him, yes, I'd say so. And a god might be supposed to have the power to intervene in extraordinary ways," said Aldous. "But God isn't a god."

"Hold on, old chap. Didn't He create everything? Isn't that the Christian understanding, anyway?"

"Is creativity the same as power?"

"Dash it all! What about the plagues of frogs and flies and the parting of the Red Sea?"

"Instructive stories of some kind? But perhaps not literal? Myths, though not in a pejorative sense? I don't know."

"Ah, well, of course as a Theosophist I always look for the Deeper Meaning!

"Now, Aldous," he continued, "let's be serious. I'm sure the Masters of the Great White Lodge have the most utterly extraordinary powers."

"I suppose so," said Aldous.

"Ah, so you agree?"

"I said I *suppose* so."

"Let's go to another talk."

"Yes, let's."

9.

"We were going to discuss the existence of evil, weren't we?" Aldous said to Norm.

"There are several views about this, but little agreement. We don't know everything."

"Ah, so you admit that you don't know everything?" sneered Humbert.

"I don't *know* much at all. I'm just a little koala. Although," he added, "I am a particularly wise one."

"The unfolding of possibilities would in itself involve the unforeseen," nudged Aldous.

"We think it's because the Great Spirit Koala wants to love koalas and for them to love the Great Spirit Koala. And if koalas were to be free – to love, above all else – there had to be elements of possibility and chance... and of course freedom to choose one thing rather than another. Otherwise we'd be... I believe you call such things 'machines'."

"Yes," said Aldous, "robots."

"I don't know that word," said Norm.

"I don't understand any of this," said Humbert to Aldous. "The Great Spirit Koala has a funny way of loving koalas, allowing bush fires and Aboriginal hunters to occur...."

"I'm not sure I completely understand. I think he believes the Great Spirit Koala allows various possibilities to unfold, but only wishes some of them. In order for koalas to act freely and with a range of possible scenarios, there has to be free will, and there has to be chance."

"Yes," said Norm. "There had to be all these possibilities! The Great Spirit Koala didn't *want* evil to happen, but it had to be part of the unfolding of possibilities."

"But surely koalas are very simple creatures?" queried Humbert. "Do they even have free will? I mean, they're not humans!"

"You don't seem to be listening at all!" exclaimed Norm.

"And good and evil? How do you see them?" asked Aldous.

"They're different *to the very heart.*"

Norm paused.

"Some things are more clearly evil than others. The black people who kill us for food don't think they're doing evil, though *we* do. But what people who start bushfires do, that's more evil, whatever *they* think. And the

Catastrophe – "

"What's the Catastrophe?"

"We suffer from various... disturbances, events that disrupt our lives. But the Catastrophe was possibly the single worst thing that happened to us. We were taken by force from our native land and made to live in a dark, cramped hold in a ship for many months, with little to eat or drink. Some had been injured or killed during the capture. Many died during our time on board. Terrible separations choked us. And then we were taken to a large wire enclosure on land, where we were jeered at and threatened and hit. Finally we rebelled and escaped. But I don't know how many survived... most likely few."

"Let's get this straight," said Aldous. "Is good the opposite of evil?"

"It's not so much what you people call an 'opposite', as utterly distinct. Opposites are apt to shade into each other. If you think in terms of opposites, dark by degrees becomes light, light becomes dark. But good doesn't become evil, or evil good. Opposites are related."

"So they're distinct, but not opposites?" Aldous ventured.

"I'd guess you could say they're contrasts," said Norm.

"They're contraries," said Humbert. "We're talking about contraries!"

"I suppose you could just say they're distinct from each other. Variously distinct. Extremely distinct in some cases," offered Aldous. "With contraries we're still talking about opposites."

"Don't put words into his mouth," said Humbert.

"They're distinct," said Norm. He suddenly batted his furry ears and then scratched his side with one of his feet.

"Why did you do that?" asked Humbert.

"I felt like it."

"You don't have fleas, do you?" asked Aldous.

"No. And please don't be so rude."

"Sorry, old chap."

"Is there *really* a difference? Can't good and evil be distinct from each other and also opposites?" asked Humbert irritably.

"Oh dear! You really are in need of koala wisdom. If one thing is known by its opposite, we might even say *exists* because of its opposite, then good is dependent upon evil for its very existence, or at any rate our knowledge of it."

"Sophistry!" exclaimed Humbert.

"Oh, I don't know," said Aldous. "Let him continue, Humbert, please."

"Good is not created by koalas, or by any other creatures. It comes from – "

"The Great Spirit Koala?" suggested Aldous.

"Yes."

"So good can't shade into evil, or evil into good?"

"That would be impossible."

Norm yawned.

"Let's go for a walk, Humbert," said Aldous, "and let Norm sleep for a while."

10.

"If he's identifying the Good with the Divine, as I think he is, then the Good can't be diluted, though it can be reflected more or less perfectly or imperfectly," said Aldous, succumbing to capitals.

"Dash it all, Aldous! Isn't that the same thing?"

"No, old chap. Dilution and reflection are different processes and different metaphors."

Aldous thought for a moment.

"I suspect good and evil are what would make a system impossible for him. Other things he's talked about might just be made into a system, though perhaps he wouldn't agree. But good and evil are what break the whole thing into fragments."

"Would he really see it that way?"

"Let's find out."

11.

"Is that furry little bugger awake yet? It's been sixteen hours!"

"I've heard they can sleep for as long as twenty-two hours on a trot."

"Every time the little bugger seems to be coming to some sort of point or other, he falls asleep! Perhaps I should throw some water over him and wake him up?"

"That would be unkind," said Aldous.

Just then Norm woke. "Where was I?" he asked.

"We were still discussing good and evil," said Aldous.

"Good is what evil isn't. Evil is what good isn't."

"But not opposites?"

"No. Not opposites."

"You mean *other than?*"

"That sounds right," said Norm. "It isn't *like* it *at all*. It's not a matter of degrees. Good is 'other than' – utterly distinct. It's unlike like, and unlike unlike."

"Don't the relations between things create the overall structure?" asked Aldous.

"Doesn't the structure make the relations?" said Humbert.

"What's a 'structure'?" asked Norm.

"A structure is where things are related – "

"Ah! Like branches."

" – into an organised whole. We also use the word 'system' where the organisation refers to something other than an object."

"Oh!"

Aldous tried to explain it to him.

"Ah," said Norm, "that's something other than branches."

"You mean branching, let's call it, in your sense at least, is something open, not closed into a whole."

Norm nodded.

"Systems can be subject to change. But they'd still have to close themselves off in some way; or be closed off," Aldous mused.

"Opposites are related. Yes, I suppose that could be held to be true."

"They're part of the same system, therefore on the same level?"

"Systems again!" exclaimed Norm. "Good and evil are *un*-related. That's my understanding."

"But there's no system here!" exclaimed Humbert.

"Why should there be?" asked Norm, indignantly.

He paused, then continued:

"When you look up into bright sunlight, do you know its brightness because of the night? When it's dark in the bush, when the dark fills all the trees, do you know this because of the sun?"

"But there's shade at the same time as sunlight," Aldous countered.

"Do I know one *because* of the other?"

"Let's take another example – rough and smooth." Aldous searched amongst the stones at his feet.

"Yes, you see, *this* is a rough stone. You could hurt your paws on this. And *this* one is smooth – you could tread on it fairly safely."

"I see," said Norm. He looked around at other stones on the ground. "What about this one?"

"Ah, good! Yes, this is *less* smooth than the one we just looked at, and *less* rough than the first. Or you could say it's *more* smooth than the first, and *less* smooth than the second."

"So it's really both smooth *and* rough, or neither smooth *nor* rough."

"No, no —"

"What about this one?"

"Ah, that one's smooth, but it has sharp edges. As well as rough and smooth, there's also sharp and dull. You must know this, little fellow."

"So *this* one is smooth, but it will also hurt a koala's paws?"

"Well, yes —"

"And what about a rough stone, a sharp stone, a dull stone and a smooth stone, all of which have been under a strong sun for hours. Would all of them hurt a koala's paws?"

"Yes – "

"So why not just use two 'categories', as I believe you call them – 'hurtful-to-paws' and 'not-hurtful-to-paws'?"

"Damn it," interrupted Humbert, "a stone when it's hot and when it's cold is still the same stone!"

"*Is* it?" said Norm. "Something burns the paws and something doesn't, and yet it's the same thing?"

"Aldous, let's face it, his is a koala-centred universe."

"What's wrong with that?" Norm asked. "Is a human-centred world better in any way?"

Humbert ignored him.

"What about wet and dry?" asked Aldous. "Surely there's a great difference for you between a pool with much water and one with little and especially one with none."

"Koalas think of them as 'good-for-drinking' or 'no-good-for-drinking'. Shallow water is good as long as it lasts. As good as a pool with a lot of water."

"Let's try something else. What if the water is too hot to drink or if it's cool?"

"If it's too hot, we'd wait until evening."

"Yes, but – "

"It would be 'water-you-could-drink' or 'water-you-couldn't-drink'."

Norm paused and then began again.

"When a joey, straying from his or her mother, innocently approaches a camp fire and reaches out its paw and almost burns itself – does it feel that painful burning heat *because* of a contrast with cold? Does it feel pain *because* of a contrast with pleasure?"

"So it doesn't actually burn itself?"

"It would have to be a very stupid joey for that to happen."

"I tried to touch a flame once when I was a child and burned myself…," Humbert began and then stopped.

Norm nodded.

"Isn't the contrast what establishes those things?"

"No, *they* give us the contrast."

"Yes, but – "

"I'm going to take a nap," interrupted Norm.

"Yes, all right, go to sleep," said Humbert.

......

"Do you think he's applying Occam's razor, or at least some strange marsupial version of it?"

"Applying *what?*"

"You know, not multiplying entities when it's unnecessary to do so."

"I'd like to apply a razor to *him.*"

"You don't really mean that, Humbert old boy!"

"You're right, I don't. Well, I might just shave off some of that ear fur...."

12.

 "Perhaps a spirit or a form of life allows – permits – a structure, and the structure allows that spirit to continue," Humbert conjectured.

Norm woke up, stretched, yawned and scratched himself.

"Oh, structures again!

"I suppose a koala's bones might be what you call a structure, but that's not a koala. Even the things inside our skins and bones... even if that's what you mean, it's not a koala."

"Isn't it?" asked Aldous, intrigued. He leaned forwards.

"No, it's just bones and what's under the skin."

Norm yawned.

"I need to sleep some more," he said, then promptly curled up and was indeed asleep in no time, right where he was.

"When he talks about branches, and clusters of branches, isn't he really speaking about structures?" Aldous conjectured. "Very open structures, but somehow still structures?"

"Aldous, he's a *koala*. It's amazing we can understand anything at all of what he says. It should be utterly unintelligible."

"But it isn't!"

13.

"Sunlight and moonlight don't mix together," said Norm. "The sun shines, and the moon and the stars shine. What I like best is a warm sunny day with a cool breeze."

"But light and darkness – " began Humbert.

"I think he's saying that's the wrong comparison," said Aldous.

"What about male and female, then? Surely we're still talking about opposites?

"Are female koalas the opposite of you males?"

"No, of course not. They're different, of course: they have pouches, they give birth, and so on. But if anything is our opposite, it's your kind – most of you, anyway."

"Do the females complement you males?"

"Some do; but then some males complement other males: and that's nothing to do with mating."

"Sex," said Aldous, "we'd say: as a more general term."

"Mating. Sex. Is there a difference? Not for us."

"There's a distinction – for humans; in as much as sex isn't always about trying to create babies."

"Ah well."

"What about your lovers – your sexual partners?"

"I don't tell those sort of stories," said Norm.

He paused.

"Actually, my mum was the first Extraordinary Koala I ever encountered, long before I went on my travels. But I didn't realise it until recently. I remember how my mum – "

"What was her name?" asked Aldous.

"Florence. She looked after me lovingly and selflessly. Her love for me was the first I knew of love; and meditating upon this, it gave me an insight into the Great Spirit Koala's love for all koalas."

Aldous asked, "Does the Great Spirit Koala love us, as well?"

"Let's not get carried away! But I'm sure you could learn from koala wisdom and be better humans."

"Impertinent beastie!" exclaimed Humbert.

Norm jumped onto a rock and stared up at him, right in the eyes.

"All this about good and evil and so forth! Balderdash! Mere semantics!" Humbert spat out.

"They're not on the same plane? Good and evil, I mean, if Humbert really wants to return to the matter. Not part of the same system?" volunteered Aldous.

"You're a Dualist!" said Humbert. "A Manichean, a Parsee...."

"A *what?*" queried Norm. He looked as puzzled as a koala can look.

"No," said Aldous, "if good and evil aren't part of the same system, surely that's not Dualism."

"Ah, I begin to see now – I like the paradoxes!" said Humbert.

"Fool," said Norm.

"*What?!*"

"And *the disturbance?*" Aldous asked, hoping that he could distract Humbert and Norm.

"There've been many disturbances."

"But *the Catastrophe?*"

"It mattered. Of course it did. But it was a disturbance, nothing else."

"That sounds somewhat callous, old chap."

"Of course they suffer! I don't take their suffering lightly, nor should you. And what good does their suffering bring? But hopefully they realise, either before or when or after they die, that they're embraced by the Great Spirit Koala, and by all the koalas past and present and future."

He paused.

"And don't forget, the Catastrophe affected me, too."

He paused again.

"I'm feeling sleepy," he said and yawned.

"Let's go for a walk, Humbert," said Aldous. "Let Norm sleep for a while."

14.

"Perhaps we need to map what's there – I mean the real, the actual – by structures and systems, until we reach something that goes beyond such mapping?" suggested Aldous.

"Yes, but is that what *he's* saying?"

"Well, he *is* just a little koala, even if a very unusual one."

Norm woke then.

"Hang it all, I still don't see clearly about contraries and about systems," said Humbert.

"No," said Aldous, "I have some questions as well."

"Do you know black because of white, or do you see black in relation to blue or yellow and white in relation to red or brown or green?"

He paused for a moment.

"Red sunsets, green leaves, brown hills... blue skies, yellow feathers or white... black of utter night: we see all these. The sky can be blue to black, but including green or red, rather than white to black. Then there are clouds against blue..."

He paused.

"There's the gray of a pigeon and the gray of a stone...."

"You don't by any chance have a colour wheel on you?" asked Aldous.

"Now what would I be doing with a colour wheel, Aldous?"

"Could you do him a drawing, then? You know, gradations of black to grey to white?"

"Oh, very well."

"Ah, perhaps each is distinct from one another from moment to moment...."

"I suppose you're going to deny time next?" sneered Humbert.

"Why on earth would I do that?" asked Norm, looking as puzzled as a koala can.

He resumed:

"Yes, bright sunlight is one thing, night's darkness is another, and sunshine and shade together is yet another."

"Aren't darkness and light *opposed*?"

"They're the same thing, really," said Norm. "What's wrong with darkness?"

"Extraordinary!"

"Koalas like the night. They come down from their trees and wander about. But they sometimes do the same in the daytime."

"You clearly don't mind being around in the daylight," said Aldous.

"No."

Norm paused.

"Beyond your 'contraries' there is an entire world."

"Yes, but what does it all add up to?"

"It doesn't. Everything finds its place in relation to the Great Spirit Koala and gains by "going into", returning to, the Great Spirit Koala. It becomes more itself – *regains* itself."

He paused briefly.

"This is the Great Spirit Koala's gift. But we have to accept it. And that's not always easy."

"But couldn't all this simply be what it is? And because it is?" asked Aldous. "Do you have to bring a Great Spirit Koala into it at all?"

Norm looked indignant, as far as a koala can. "Do you think a stone is what it is because it is what it is, and a koala is what he or she is because he or she is what he or she is?"

"Ah, I guess."

"We didn't *bring* the Great Spirit Koala into 'it'. The Great Spirit Koala precedes everything and makes it possible."

He paused.

"It's in spirit dreams that I find myself there – where all this becomes clear to me."

"Are *we* going to rely on *his* dreams?" scoffed Humbert.

"This is all reflected in nature and other koalas – for example, the way a koala will sometimes look at another," said Norm.

"Tell me, you *really* are an Adept, aren't you?" said Humbert, changing tack.

"If you *really* think I might be, why do you keep making fun of me?"

"Because if you're not an Adept, it means you're just a koala."

"What's wrong with being a koala?"

"Well, a koala is hardly a human being, for one thing."

"And what's so wonderful about being human?"

"You clearly think you're superior," said Humbert accusingly.

Norm looked hurt and indignant, as far as a koala can.

"I feel hurt and indignant," he said. "It's not my fault you humans are so lacking in wisdom and so ready to hurt and kill."

"Your English really *is* good!" said Aldous.

"So you keep telling me. I admit I've worked on it quite a lot."

"I wish you'd stop being so testy," said Aldous to Humbert. "The little chap's doing his best to tell us how and what he thinks. This is really an extraordinary occasion."

"Yes, I suppose so."

"And perhaps he *does* have something to teach us."

"I do," said Norm.

Aldous turned to Norm.

"Would you prefer it if we talked in terms of 'patterns'?"

"Ah, yes! I know that word."

He looked at them both for a long while.

"... as long as you see that patterns melt into larger patterns, as well as into smaller: until a pattern isn't visible any more. Within, sometimes, without, sometimes, they can seem limitless, and perhaps are."

"I don't think you're paying attention to the way we have to interpret things," said Aldous. "For example, you might see a long greyish-brown shape in a river, and some might see it as a log, and others as an alligator...."

"I've heard about alligators from other koalas – Extraordinary Koalas, who have travelled far more than I. You'd have to be pretty stupid to mistake an alligator for a log."

"But it's possible! And it was only an example."

"For once I have to agree with our furry interlocutor, Aldous, although my objection is a little different than his. Of course we can make mistakes about what we see, or see one thing as something and then as something else, but you can't generalise too much from these cases, old boy. In fact, they may well be the exceptions that prove the rule."

"Aren't they a little more common than that?"

"Oh, I don't think so, old chap."

"But what rule are you talking about, Humbert?"

"That our senses don't usually deceive us and that we don't have to make choices between seeing one thing or another thing."

"Humbert, I can't believe you're saying this! You're a Theosophist! You don't think perception involves a processing of raw sensory data –?"

"Aldous, surely you don't favour that empiricist 'raw sensory data' nonsense?"

"It does seem to fit in with what we know scientifically, old chap."

"Oh, the scientists will come round on this, just as they will about reincarnation and auras. My being a Theosophist doesn't preclude having good old common sense. Oh, I know there are Theosophists who believe that what we normally see is an illusion. But they're wrong. It's just that there's also *a lot more* than what we normally see and experience and know. Not everyone sees auras, anymore than everyone is able to receive messages from the Great White Lodge: just to give you an idea, old chap."

"Or remember past lives, for that matter?"

"Of course, Aldous; of course: exactly right."

"Let me try something else out. When people who have been blind from birth have an operation that allows them to see for the first time, they're initially confused – they can't sort out and make sense of what appears in their visual field."

"A special case, old boy, from which you can't generalise too much: something you tend to do, I'm afraid. They're like a small child, without the adult's 'tuning', but with expectations a child doesn't have."

" 'Tuning'?"

"I'm willing to admit that perception involves a successive tuning and re-tuning of what we see, but which still remains fundamentally direct."

"Aren't you contradicting yourself, Humbert?"

"Oh, I don't think so, old chap."

"You don't think perception is a matter of – "

"Aldous, you're obviously going to go on about sensation and perception, and then about experience."

"Could I get back to telling you about koala wisdom?" asked Norm.

"By the way, Humbert," said Aldous, "I do sometimes wish we didn't sound like university graduates."

"Why? That's exactly what we are."

"I won't even ask," said Norm, looking somewhat impatient: as far as a koala can. "Excuse me, but can I continue now?"

"Yes, of course, old chap," said Aldous.

Norm gestured upwards with his paw, above his head, and then to himself.

"Cliché!" exclaimed Humbert.

"Extraordinary," said Aldous. "He's saying what many religious teachers and mystics have said. 'The Kingdom of Heaven is within you and without you': inside and outside, within and beyond. Transcendence... and immanence. The transcendent is also the immanent, and the immanent the transcendent. And he's a *koala!*"

"What?" queried Norm. " 'Transcendence' and...?"

"Oh, you wouldn't understand!" said Humbert. "Despite what Aldous thinks." He turned to his friend. "But Aldous, isn't *that* a cliché, too?"

"I'm not sure it isn't true, though. Or let's say: actual. I have a feeling – "

"You have a *feeling?*"

"Yes. Could it be that what goes beyond also goes far within: within ourselves and also in some sense within nature."

"Why don't you let him tell it, Aldous?"

"It's about going beyond and going deep within," said Norm.

"So then it's a relationship to the Beyond?"

"But let's not capitalise it," said Aldous.

"How did you know...?"

"I guessed. 'What's beyond,' let's say. But how do we have a relationship to... what's beyond the relational?"

"We have it because we're Adepts... *if* we're Adepts!"

"That's begging the question, old boy."

"Perhaps the Absolute is Absolute in itself and relative in everything?"

"It's not a thing amongst things?"

"Of course not."

"But can we still say that the relative is relative to the Absolute?"

"Why not?"

"Aren't we back at opposites?"

"Oh," said Norm, "we're talking about distinctions, if I understand the word!" He nodded. "I'm going to take a nap."

"Damn him and his bloody naps!" exclaimed Humbert. "I'd exclude *him*!"

"Why have you become so antagonistic towards the little chap?"

"Because he's an utter know-it-all, that's why."

Aldous picked Norm up and gave him a cuddle.

"I've grown rather fond of him," he said. "By George, I think I sense that he wants to subvert what we call systems, or be enslaved by one system or another."

"You infuriating marsupial!" Humbert exclaimed, looking at Norm. "I wish you didn't sound so persuasive."

"I'm not persuasive. I'm right. I'm wise."

"How on earth did you arrive at all this?"

"I went to a koala academy, a place where koalas learn from each other. I met many Extraordinary Koalas."

"Ah, an academy! A Koala Academy!"

"But it's more to do with dreams, visions, meditation, insight."

15.

"But the Absolute surely must be undifferentiated," said Aldous, continuing the discussion later that day.

"What's he on about?" asked Norm, stirring from his sleep.

"Well, he's talking about the relative and the Absolute as opposites...."

"Oh, dear! *Opposites* again!"

"I wondered what our furry friend would say," said Humbert.

"I guess we have!" said Aldous.

"Let me tell you about my experiences. If I slipped for a moment on a tree branch, it would be like that. Not quite, though. *Startled* or *astonished*? Yes. No: not quite. What wasn't right, somehow was; what was ordinary wasn't, and yet was still itself. Suddenly? Yes. Everything seemed at rest and at peace with everything else."

His head began to nod.

"...and... and harmony... in every... the tree... the leaves...."

"Is he going into a trance?"

"I think the little fellow's just falling asleep," said Aldous.

Norm woke with a jolt.

"There was a sense of order and harmony, peace and goodness... spread throughout... with everything falling into place....until everything was made of light, and everything *was* light. And everything was embraced by the Great Spirit Koala."

"Did you feel at one with the Great Spirit Koala?"

"Oh, yes!"

"Did you feel that you *were* the Great Spirit Koala?"

Norm looked at them askance, or at least as far as a koala can.

"Don't be silly!" he exclaimed. "What a ridiculous question! You humans really are in need of wisdom."

"What about 'the eye with which I see God is the same as the eye with which God sees me'? A great mystic said that.'

Norm came as close to frowning as a koala can, and then yawned. "I think I'll take a nap," he said.

16.

"Presumably the Great Spirit Koala knows everything?"

"The Great Spirit Koala is the source of knowledge, but if you mean, for example, does the Great Spirit Koala know English or not, you're asking a silly question. The Great Spirit Koala isn't a human being, nor even a koala. You might as well ask if the Great Spirit Koala knows about hairdressing."

"You know about *hairdressing?*"

"Ah, yes, someone at the conference mentioned it."

"You're *that* attentive?"

"Why not? But why talk about knowledge? It's wisdom we should be talking about. The Great Spirit Koala is all-wise."

"What about power? Isn't the Great Spirit Koala all-powerful?"

"Ah, power! Yes, I know that word. It usually means violence or taking into captivity or crushing down. The Great Spirit Koala is creative, not powerful in your sense! And we koalas are called upon to be like the Great Spirit Koala. Not all respond to the call, unfortunately."

"Isn't the Great Spirit Koala everything?"

"The Great Spirit Koala allows the appearance of separation to happen. It all dissolves back into the Great Spirit Koala. The appearance seems real, it *feels* real, it can't be ignored or dismissed. It *is* real. The Great Spirit Koala isn't evil, and the Great Spirit Koala isn't human beings. But in the end, the Great Spirit Koala is what's wholly and actually real.

"Oh dear," he said, "I'm so tired!"

17.

Aldous and Humbert took a stroll after having been to a long talk and discussion.

"You know, I suspect that beneath it all most of these people are really atheists," said Aldous.

"Atheism is the last refuge of those who are both spiritually blind and intellectually smug," said Humbert. "Don't be silly, Aldous."

"I was thinking more of the spiritually arrogant," replied Aldous.

"Now, come on, old boy!"

"Well, I heard talk of 'esoteric Christianity,' but no mention of Christ. Isn't mystical or visionary experience predicated on faith?"

"Oh, surely we've gone beyond that!"

"I'm not advocating anything: I'm scarcely a Christian myself. But surely Christianity has to be based on faith: that's all I'm saying."

"You of all people, Aldous!"

"Oh, I don't think I'm really all *that* cynical, despite what you think! I simply have an eye and an ear for contemporary foibles, falsehoods and self-delusions. Anyway, as I've said, I'm not talking about my own faith or beliefs."

18.

"I want to talk about individuals," Norm said.

"You know what the word 'individuals' means?" Aldous asked.

"Oh yes."

He paused.

"Do I see a koala because I know it's a koala? No, I know it's a koala because I see a koala."

"*What?!*" exclaimed Humbert.

"I think he means the perception of an individual entity precedes rather than follows on from the general concept."

"Well, he might have said so!"

"He did."

"Hrrrmph! Anyway, what does any of this matter?"

"Well, it gives a priority to the individual being or thing... an emphasis... and a dignity and importance, I suppose."

"I do wish you wouldn't speak for him, Aldous."

"Look at it this way," Aldous replied. "You're the individual Humbert J Brockenhurst before rather than after you're the species *homo sapiens*, then a man, then an Englishman, then an upper-middle-class Englishman, then an upper-middle-class male Theosophist...."

"But I'm a Great Soul before I'm anything else!" exclaimed Humbert. "Anyway, why are you speaking for him again, Aldous?"

"Because he's fallen asleep. Can't you hear him snore?"

"Oh, blast!"

......

When Norm woke, they returned to the subject of individuals.

"If you see a crowd, you don't see individuals," Aldous opted.

"Are we talking about koalas? Then a large group – a "crowd", as you call it – is a crowd of individuals."

"If you saw a large number of koalas at a distance – "

"They'd be individual koalas and I'd eventually see them as individuals. What else would they be?"

"Yes, but – "

"I might not be able to *recognise* them as particular koalas at first, but I'd see them as individuals."

"Oh, God, I do wish this little furry blighter would go away, especially as I have to admit I agree with him!"

"Now, Humbert, be nice," said Aldous. "Norm is trying to be helpful."

"That's right," said Norm. "But in your case, Humbert, I wonder if I'm wasting my time."

"Unlike Humbert, I'm afraid I don't agree with you this time. What about if the group of koalas is at such a distance they're only a blur?"

"A *what?*"

Aldous explained to Norm what a blur was.

"As long as I can actually see them as koalas, it would be a blur of individual koalas."

"I'm not sure that makes sense, old chap."

"Hang it all," exclaimed Humbert, "why do you disagree with him on the rare occasions I'm in agreement?"

"I don't know: it's certainly not deliberate. But then you just changed your mind about the whole 'individuals' thing."

"Well, I suddenly saw his point, old boy."

....

"By the way, I hope you're not an adherent of that Freud fellow's mumbo-jumbo, are you, Aldous?" Humbert said later. "I've heard you mention the 'unconscious' at times!"

"Well, I – "

"Seems like a lot of pseudo-scientific superstition to me. All those bloody complexes and envies and repressions and other balderdash: you'd have to be members of the neurotic upper-middle-class Viennese or their doctors to believe any of that nonsense!"

"Well – "

"At least the old boy doesn't seem to encourage the infantile, unlike those Surrealist chaps we've been hearing about recently."

"What I've seen of it does appear numbing and oddly predictable, I must say – either with a deliberately disordered association of images or in a heavy-handed reliance on Freudian symbolism. Limp this, upright that – animals on fire – that sort of thing."

"I couldn't have put it better myself, Aldous, though I haven't seen anything quite like that! Also, I'm not sure what would constitute light-handed Freudian symbolism."

"Ah, yes! I suppose you're right. Ha!"

"And let's not forget all that tedious 'automatic writing'!"

"No, indeed!"

19.

"I still have questions," said Aldous. "All the things you talk about.... Isn't this just the sort of raw material that scientists classify, categorise and systematise."

"Scientists?" queried Norm. "Who do *what* and *what* and *what*?"

Aldous tried to explain, at some length, with interjections from Humbert.

Norm shuddered. "Ah, I almost met some of those people. They wanted to experiment on us – the koalas at the colony. That was what finally made us revolt. But they were called 'doctors'."

"I suppose they were medical scientists, or even doctors with an amateur interest in animal anatomy. Zoologists," said Aldous.

"Vivisectionists," chimed in Humbert.

"I won't even ask," said Norm. "No doubt there would have been cruelties inflicted before we were killed. Starving us, forcing us to eat strange things, deliberately making us ill so that they could try out 'cures', perhaps even putting things in our eyes...." He shuddered again.

"I still think he's a deuced Dualist!" muttered Humbert.

"Nonsense," countered Aldous. "I think he *is* wise, but he's also naïve – like a child. Well, he's a koala, after all. I also think he may be in a state of grace."

"He may be *what?!*"

"Well, he may be *blessed*. As in the Beatitudes: 'Blessed are the peacemakers,' and so forth. Blessed are the koalas, for they are wise."

"Balderdash, Aldous!"

"Oh, I don't know..."

"Who is he? *What* is he, really?" Humbert turned from Aldous to Norm. "Admit it, even if you're not an Adept, you're some sort of superkoala!"

"I'd rather just be thought of as especially wise." He paused. "All koalas have wisdom, but some have more than others. And only a few of us can express it more or less adequately." Again he paused. "But that doesn't mean the others aren't wise as well."

"Do you feel like you're trapped in the wrong body?" asked Aldous. "I mean, that you should be a different species?"

"Certainly not. And I hope you don't mean *human?*"

"Surely knowledge and understanding are dependent on language?" asked Aldous, changing tack.

"Not in our world," said Norm.

"But you speak English..."

"I had lessons," Norm replied; "I also eavesdropped a good deal. But I knew and understood things long before that. Before I spoke a language. And we don't all. Not by any means."

"You bellow, grunt, growl...."

"You call that a language?" asked Norm rhetorically.

"I was only trying not to be condescending."

"And that's what you *are* being. By the way, I know several black people's languages as well. But I only learned them late on."

He paused.

"What you call 'language' is only possible because of the Great Spirit Koala. Whenever you say a word – or make a drawing or merely a mark on something – it's because of the Great Spirit Koala. And whenever you do, the Great Spirit Koala is there."

"Extraordinary!" exclaimed Aldous.

"It sounds to me that you koalas are in need of human language to fully communicate," sneered Humbert.

"Hardly! I'll send you a dream, and then you'll have a better idea of how we communicate."

"Hrrrmph!"

20.

"You believe in auras, thought-forms, astral projection and reincarnation, not to mention the Mahatmas of the Great White Lodge...."

"All of which will be proved by science one of these days, old chap. As far as the Mahatmas go, well, you have to be an Adept to be in touch with them, of course."

"What about the Great Furry Brotherhood and Sisterhood? Is there such a thing?" Aldous asked Norm.

"No. But there is the Communion of Koalas."

Aldous turned back to Humbert. "Tell us more about the Great White Lodge of Mahatmas. Do they love us, for instance?"

"I'm not sure they *love* us, but they're wise... and masterful... and jolly terrific."

"I'm wise," said Norm.

"Listen, pipsqueak, one more word out of you – "

"Why don't you like him?" asked Aldous. "And by the way – 'pipsqueak'? You've been listening to our American friends."

"I did like him: before he started talking! If he'd only stayed in his place, and didn't pretend to be a Master, I might still like him."

"I'm not a master," said Norm, "I'm just wise."

"*You're a little furry creature!*" shouted Humbert.

"And I'm wise," said Norm evenly.

"Do you believe in reincarnation?" Humbert explained the concept to him.

"We'd be born again *here?*"

"Why not?" said Humbert.

"Why *twice*... or *more?* Surely once is enough? I mean, you'd really want to be born here *again?* This place is all very well, the Great Spirit Koala let it happen, and it has the Great Spirit Koala's imprints – paw prints, we might say. But *again?*"

"What else would there be, furry Adept?" asked Humbert, smirking.

"I'm not an Adept, just a koala." He gestured with his paw towards himself and then above him.

"Not again!" cried Humbert.

"Amazing!" cried Aldous.

"But what else is there?" insisted Humbert,

"Don't you mean *where* else is there?"

"You could always tell us," Aldous intervened.

"We only have vague suggestions in our dreams," Norm replied. "Our spirit journeys in our dreams... and our visions... and also what we call 'seeing-into'." He paused.

"Imagine something like this place and yet not this – definitely not. Your dreams, your truest dreams, will give you some sense of what I mean."

"*Truest?*"

"Those that mean most to you and tell you something: something that lifts you up and carries you away."

"Sentimental balderdash!"

"You try to believe in what you call 'Adepts' and all the rest of it because you can't really believe in anything at all. You believe in nothing."

"I... I... I...!" stuttered Humbert.

"He might have you there," said Aldous. "If you really believed in astral planes and lotus lands and what-have-you, would you find *his* beliefs so objectionable?"

"You arrogant little twerp!" exclaimed Humbert, ignoring Aldous and pointing his finger at Norm.

Norm finally lost his temper. "I'll scratch you if you don't stop this!"

"Gentlemen! Gentlemen!" cried Aldous.

"From here," said Norm, continuing his account regardless, "you enter into something better... or worse."

He paused.

"As far as this earth goes – we believe that when the last koala has passed into the Spirit Land to be with the Great Spirit Koala, this place will dissolve into dust."

"Will we pass into the Spirit Land as well?" asked Aldous.

"I would have thought that was most unlikely. But perhaps a few of you will."

Aldous decided on a different line of questioning. "But isn't this place – this earth – a good place?"

"Yes, but there are also things I wouldn't wish on any koala. Bushfires, for one. Human violence, for another."

"I hate to admit it, but he's got us there," Humbert said, sighing; "*mutatis mutandis* we could say the same about our own lives here."

"I know, old boy. I was just interested to see what he'd say."

"Couldn't koalas go straight to the Spirit Land, without ever being here?"

"No, they have to develop freedom of choice here... or in the other places *after* this one but *before* they're ready to enter the Spirit Land."

"But didn't a great philosopher say that this is the best of all possible worlds?"

"Leibnitz, I believe," said Aldous.

"You humans can be quite mad," said Norm.

....

While Norm napped, Aldous and Humbert talked about possible worlds.

"This has got me thinking," said Humbert. "Why indeed couldn't *this* be a much better world?"

"Is it against your Theosophical beliefs to countenance such a thing?" asked Aldous.

"I don't see why it would, old chap. Now, what if we start by eliminating pain?"

"All right. I suppose various things would have to be absent from the world, such as anything sharp, or fire for another thing. There'd be no diseases. Or else the human body would have to be impervious to pain and ills and destruction. We'd be eliminating danger and risk, which would take away some of life's capacity for excitement, and I'd guess we would all end up quite complacent. Also, if there's no disease and the body's indestructible, we could live forever."

"What would be wrong with that? And surely disease is scarcely a good thing!"

"Would we age, or would we just stay the same eternally?"

"Oh, stay the same, surely."

"At what sort of age? A child? An adolescent? Someone in their prime? A more elderly person? And what about development? Would our brains and minds stay exactly the same?"

"We could be at the stage where our knowledge is perfect and we don't need to change or learn."

"Is that even possible? And what would be the challenge in that?"

"There'd be no need for it, old chap."

"So there'd be no begetting, no children, no new people? New people with different ideas?"

"Whatever for?"

"What about emotions? Would we feel emotional pain? Would our emotions develop and change?"

"No, I suppose not."

"It sounds like we'd be robots or zombies."

"No, no, we'd have reached a sort of perfection."

"Or death-in-life. Presumably we'd never experience strife, and we wouldn't feel deeply – because if we did, we might feel pain at rejection, for instance...."

"We'd always make the right choices, Aldous: that's how it might be."

"It's beginning to sound as if everything's determined for us."

"Oh, I don't believe in that determinism nonsense, old chap! My sister Ethelred has the same family, the same upbringing, the same sort of education (though in her case she was schooled privately), the same social milieu, and she's as unlike me as you might imagine! Well, you've met her, Aldous: she's a rotten egg if ever there was one, hates everyone but the other people in her silly little church, shows no kindness to anyone, in fact does her best to torment our poor Mama. Yet all the same determinants are there...."

"I suppose someone would say that to begin with there's her gender – "

"She's had all the advantages I have, old chap."

" – and there are other determinants we're simply not aware of."

"Balderdash!"

"Having been given such an odd name for a woman probably didn't help."

"She could have changed it."

"Let me try a different tack. What sort of climate would this world of yours have?"

"Oh, it would be just right: not too cold, not too hot. You know."

"But some people like it to be hot and some people like it to be cool. If it was too cold for you, you couldn't have a fire to keep you warm, because fires can be harmful – unless of course your body really is indestructible. Electricity's no good, because you might have an electrical fire."

"Oh, I'm sure there could be something else that wouldn't be potentially harmful."

"And what about rain? Crops and plants need it, and it can be pleasant for us if it's not heavy, and pleasant to watch even when it is. But you can then get flooding...."

"Surely it could be regulated, old boy. Also, Aldous, we could all like the *same* climate and weather! There'd be no reason for disagreement or dissatisfaction."

"Ah, Norman's waking up!" said Aldous.

21.

"When we koalas emerged from the coming-into-life-of-possibilities," Norm said, "the whole thing reached its peak and ultimate purpose – at least as far as this earth goes. We were the very mirror image of the Great Spirit Koala!

"Each and every koala is sacred," he continued. "Well, I think I'll take a nap now."

"Before you do, can you tell us this: are we sacred, too?" Aldous asked.

"I do wish you two wouldn't keep asking silly questions," replied Norm. "I really will take a nap now."

And he was soon fast asleep.

"This little furry know-it-all – "

"I don't think he's a 'know-it-all,' Humbert. He feels that he can see into the heart of things. Or so I'd say. And surely that's what wisdom's all about."

When Norm woke again, Aldous prompted him:

"You were telling us about your experiences of harmony and peace..."

"Oh, that's just the beginning! You have to go on spirit journeys, you have to listen to the Great Spirit Koala...."

"Would we be able to do these things?"

"Probably not. Accept what's possible for you."

"Piffle!" said Humbert.

"Extraordinary!" said Aldous. "But can you give us an example of one of your visions?"

"I once saw an enormous tree, and a voice, a very sweet voice, came distinctly from the top.... 'Climb,' the voice seemed to tell me, although there were no words, 'climb'.

"And so I did. It took me ever so long to reach near to the top branches. And there I was blinded – it may sound strange, but whether by light or by darkness I couldn't tell. Either there was a bright flare followed by darkness, or the sudden intensity of the dark blinded me as if by bright light. However, I kept looking, and gradually I saw the form of an enormous koala – yet every time I saw a little of it more distinctly, it vanished again into the darkness."

"I've had Great Spiritual Experiences," said Humbert. "I've had messages from the Masters of the White Lodge. I've woken in the morning to find pieces of paper with writing on them, telling me I'm an Adept."

"Are you sure you didn't write those things yourself when you were drunk, old boy?" asked Aldous. "You are fond of a tipple, you know."

"Don't be impertinent!"

"Sorry, Humbert old chap."

"You call that a great spiritual experience?" asked Norm, in lower case.

"I've never seen a giant koala, if that's what you mean!"

"I thought you said the Great Spirit Koala – " began Aldous.

"Yes, of course. But the experience was very real, just the same."

"It *seemed* very real?"

"No, it *was* very real."

"Ah, so the negations and the affirmations are not contradictory – just as in Dionysius the Areopagite!"

"Who? What?"

"Go to sleep, old boy. Humbert and I have a lot to talk about."

22.

"We've decided that what you've been telling us about... well, it's just not for us, old chap."

"Is that all you can say?" Norm looked saddened. "I've tried to give you koala wisdom."

"It may be fine for koalas, but we're humans."

Norm turned to Aldous. "You could always write about our wisdom," he said.

"No one would ever believe me if I told your story! What would be the good of writing about it? And look here, you're a koala, we can't generalise from *your* experience – "

"But from your own?"

"Aldous, I'm so tired of this furry little critter! He has an answer for almost everything."

Aldous ignored this; but he addressed Norm:

"It wouldn't work, old chap."

There was silence. Norman looked as if close to despair – as much as a koala can.

"I don't suppose either of you could help me?" he finally managed to say.

"In what way?" asked Aldous.

"I really need a home," said Norm. "Somewhere safe. With a eucalyptus tree."

"I'm afraid I can't help you," said Humbert. "If I wanted a pet, I'd get a bulldog."

Aldous shuddered. "Don't mention bulldogs," he said obscurely.

"Oh, sorry, old man!" said Humbert, none the wiser.

"*A pet!*" exclaimed Norm. "You humans!"

"At least pets don't argue with you."

Norm looked beseechingly at Aldous, at least as far as a koala can.

"Very sorry, old chap," said Aldous.

"I thought you liked me," Norm said.

"I do," replied Aldous. "But not enough to take you home, I'm afraid. And I don't have a eucalyptus tree."

"Well, then, could you help me to get back to my homeland?"

"To *Australia?*" queried Humbert.

Norm nodded, looking from one to the other.

They both shook their heads.

"What about a *zoo?*" ventured Aldous. He explained what a zoo was, with its cages and its various captive denizens and its noisy visitors.

Norm looked heartbroken – crushed.

"Oh no," he said; "no."

....

Norm looked back over his shoulder. "At least tell that ugly bald person he should call his memoirs 'Encounters With Not Very Extraordinary Men'!" he called to Humbert and Aldous. And he scampered off.

....

Norman stood on the bank. His heart beat fast.

"Here we go again," he said, and dove in.

Part Two

1.

To continue Norman's story, I have to tell you my own... and Dorothea's.

2.

"Why hello, Denis."

As I often did, I had come to the park to sit on a bench and absorb myself in a book. I looked up from my reading: Dorothea was standing before me.

I said hello.

Dorothea was my second cousin, that is, cousin to my late father. She was considered one of the family's black sheep, but I liked her. She'd always struck me as exceedingly gentle and good-natured. "Pure" perhaps doesn't work as a description; "grace" in the most serious sense is a word that comes to mind, though. And she also seemed curiously passive. If my mother or father had said she couldn't stay with us, as she sometimes asked – they were always reluctant, but did occasionally give in – she scarcely ever protested: she seemed resigned. I remember one occasion when she stayed, my mother told me not to use a certain towel because Dorothea had just used it and she was "dirty". I was somewhat puzzled, but more disgusted than anything else: not at Dorothea; rather, momentarily, at Mum.

She sat down beside me, and took out a packet of cigarettes and a box of matches from her handbag.

"What are you reading?" she asked.

"Oh, some poetry," I said.

"Oh, poetry." She opened the packet. "Would you like a cigarette?"

"No, thank you, I don't smoke."

"Ah. I thought perhaps I'd never seen you smoke because neither Bert nor Flora allowed it." She cupped her hands to light her cigarette.

"How old are you now, Denis?" she asked, exhaling smoke through her nostrils.

"Twenty-one," I lied.

"Then you could buy me a drink," she said.

....

Dorothea shook out her long honey-coloured hair.

"I love the smell of cigars," she said, commenting on someone smoking at the next table. "A pity you don't smoke, Denis. But I don't suppose you'd smoke cigars, anyway. Would you buy me one?"

"Yes," I said.

I went to the bar and came back with fresh drinks, as well as her cigar: which she lit and puffed on contentedly, her eyes closed. I was overcome. Shy as I was, I impulsively leaned over across the table and kissed her on the lips.

"Denis!" she said; then she kissed my mouth.

.....

"May I kiss you?" she asked.

I was surprised: we'd kissed a number of times at the pub and on the way to her place.

"Oh yes," I said.

She dropped to her knees and unzipped my trousers.

"Oh!" I said.

"Is this all right?" she asked.

"Oh yes," I said.

......

We lay naked in bed together. I was caressing Dorothea's breast.

"This is so nice. But I don't suppose we should be doing it."

"It's scarcely against the law," I replied.

"I'm sure Bert wouldn't have approved: I was his cousin, after all. As for Flora – my, how she'd be shocked: I'd certainly never be invited to your home again if she knew."

"Mum doesn't have to know," I said. "You're lovely, Dorothea. I want this to go on and on."

"*How* lovely, would you say?"

"As lovely as a koala."

"Hmm."

"I mean it as a supreme compliment."

She laughed. "Oh, all right, then."

I'd always thought that koalas were beautiful, of course.

– This was before the dreams began and Norm entered into our lives.

3.

At this time I was working in a modest yet very good bookshop in Oxford Circus. I was the youngest and least senior member of staff. After the owner, Zack, the most senior member was Rollo Rodney. I give his full name here because he was a well known avant-garde artist and musician. You might have heard of him.

Rollo was small, spare and fey, a little like an elfin Irish spirit or a Science Fiction character – a strange little man from Outer Space. In other words, he scarcely seemed human – or real.

"Mr Rodney," a woman said. "Mr Rodney, help me choose a book."

He attracted a certain female type – rich, bored suburban housewives with a longing for something intellectual. Mostly they came from Belgravia, Knightsbridge, Chelsea, Kensington and Mayfair, or in some instances from Hampstead. The shop had a reputation, specialising as it did in books on art and architecture, literary first editions and sheet music of a certain kind, but also small and select displays of contemporary fiction and poetry.

I always assumed Rollo was gay, though I never asked him and never had any direct confirmation of this.

He still lived at home with his parents. I still lived with my mother, but I was 18 and Rollo must have been at least twice my age.

......

When I told my friends that I was going to work at the bookshop, a couple of them said that they knew Rollo a little and that I should mention their names to him: and so I did, on the first day. "I see," he said, giving me a quizzical sidelong glance. He didn't speak to me again for a fortnight or so, apart from perfunctory instructions.

One day I came to the shop with a copy of Calvin Tomkins' *The Bride and Her Bachelors* under my arm. It was a popular introduction to a number of avant-garde artists and composers, including Marcel Duchamp and John Cage. Rollo noticed. "I'm beginning to change my mind about you," he said.

A few days later I said to him: "Art isn't therapy, Rollo." I'd been reading Alan Watts, who was very critical of Cage and used a similar phrase against him. Rollo gave a snort. "I keep changing my mind about you," he said.

....

Rollo was a materialist, like most Conceptual artists, but unlike many of them, he was not a Marxist. (– It always seemed curious and ironic that an art movement that laid so much emphasis on "dematerialisation" should be practised by materialists; the emphasis on the conceptual was often largely or even entirely at the expense of the concrete: typewritten pages, nondescript photos, and so on: documentation, instructions for performance, ideas for art, but rarely anything like painting, sculpture or printmaking.)

I'd gone on a demonstration against the Vietnam War, marching through the streets of central London. Rollo wouldn't come. Unlike the notorious riots that broke out in Grosvenor Square following an anti-war march a couple of years earlier, there was no violence. But as I found out later, the Communist Party had managed to get their members at the front, waving their flags and singing 'Over the Hills for Uncle Ho.' I was too far back to have realised that they'd grabbed the credit for what was essentially a non-party protest. (– Not that it really benefited them, mind you: all the media outlets – radio, TV, newspapers – had managed to ignore the event.)

"See," said Rollo when I later told him. "I was right to stay home and work." He paused. "At least they were on a march: that's something, I suppose. Most Western Marxists can't say or write a word unless they're in a comfortable armchair. You have to get out of your armchair to march."

"We're talking about Communists."

"There's a difference?"

"You're thinking of the middle-class or upper-middle-class intellectuals. What about working-class Communists?"

"Yes, well, you're right, I suppose. I am thinking of the arrogant little fools who feel guilty about their social background and end up trying to organise, speak for and lead the workers, usually from the safe distance of their armchairs: issuing proclamations, directives, manifestos... not to mention unintelligible poems."

Maoism was all the rage at the time amongst many artists and intellectuals. Rollo was not impressed.

"Mao's supposed to have solved the problem of drug addiction in China by rounding up the addicts and bumping them off," I remember him saying to a visitor to the bookshop, a well known painter who had brought up the problem of illegal drug usage: something that had recently been in the news. "Not that he did it personally, of course. You're not advocating anything of that sort, are you?"

"Well, it did work," the painter replied.

Rollo gave a sort of febrile laugh followed by a snort.

....

As well as being a Conceptual artist, Rollo was recognised as a musician and composer who played and wrote for the bass sax. Why he chose the bass sax was a mystery, as it's a cumbersome instrument with a very deep sound and hardly anything has been written for it. Possibly the only previous player of note was Adrian Rollini, a colleague and friend of Bix Beiderbecke and Frankie Trumbauer, but Rollo had no interest in early jazz. Rollo's playing was usually frenetic and abstract – amelodic, non-linear, and unconventionally rhythmic. I think the very absurdity of using such an instrument for his purposes was precisely what interested Rollo.

I initially thought of Webern – but Webern is seldom really frenetic, nor as thoroughly non-linear, and his music has a spirituality that Rollo's didn't. At least not for me. John Cage with his chance procedures would perhaps be a better reference point.

I played the clarinet. Rollo wasn't interested. 'Boo-hoo,' I suppose.

4.

There is a photograph by Brassaï that reminds me of Dorothea: but *why?* The photo is of a young couple in a café or bar, sitting by themselves. The woman is facing the camera. She holds a lit cigarette in an upraised hand, and she is smiling or possibly laughing. In her face I read abandonment... abandonment to love, to an affair. Dorothea on the other hand had in a sense abandoned herself. Also, she never looked as vivacious as the young woman, at least not in my experience, and she was older. But that quality of *abandonment* is the key to the resemblance.

Apart from his slicked-down hair you only see the young man through his reflection in a mirror behind the woman. He looks handsome, charming... but with cold eyes, hard eyes... dead eyes, even. He is, I'd suspect, a louse: someone who is devoted – abandoned, if you like – only to himself; and so not at all like the young woman, and nothing like Dorothea.

Or like me, I dare say. I'm not handsome and I don't try to be charming. I certainly don't try to fool anyone. I aim to be good, but don't always succeed. *I fail.* I really fail in so many things and so many ways.

....

I worried that Dorothea didn't eat enough. And her eyes were always glassy, her gaze hazy, something I'd always observed but never been sure about: now I knew she was habitually drunk or hung over, though otherwise she carried it well. She lived on little else than alcohol – white wine, brandy, whiskey, sometimes beer, even cider.

I wondered how she could afford her room, small as it was and in the area known as the Angel Islington, a rather squalid suburb. She didn't have a job and definitely didn't have an inheritance, and I knew she was sometimes homeless: after all, Flora, and Bert in past times, had reluctantly put her up now and again.

"Ask me no questions," she said, smiling, when I asked.

I'd also heard she was sometimes reduced to picking up cigarette stubs in the street to smoke. But perhaps Flora and Bert had just made this up. Why? It wasn't that my parents were mean-spirited or spiteful: not in the least. But as I've said, Dorothea was considered a black sheep – something that needs justifying.

I continued to wonder about all the streets she'd wandered and what she'd had to do to survive. What had led her to this? I never felt I could ask: it was always too much to ask.

As I've said, Dorothea drank seriously, and so did I. I won't say it was her fault that I was drinking: it wasn't; but she did influence me. Holding on to my job eventually became difficult. I suppose you could say I'd joined the ranks of functioning alcoholics, though I often arrived late and took more sick days than anyone else. Zack was tolerant. Rollo took to shaking his head in disapproval, but he rarely said anything.

. . . .

I'd written something, and I showed it to Dorothea:

84

STIGMATA

They bleed. My paws bleed, said the koala.

Mine bleed, too, said the bear. The blood flows, it pours. It trickles at first, then....

And mine – my paws bleed, said the lion. They bleed.

Mine also, said the lynx; and so also said the orang-utan and the sloth.

They bleed. My wing tips bleed, said the puffin.

As do mine, said the jay and the nuthatch and the sparrow. Yes, ours do, too, said the pigeon and the raven. And mine, said the hawk.

They bleed. My hoofs bleed, said the gazelle.

As do ours, said the zebra, the deer, the antelope and the giraffe.

The stigmata unites us all, said St Francis.

"What does it mean?" Dorothea asked when I'd finished.

"I'm not sure myself. I guess it's about how we're all bound up together in suffering."

"Hmm."

....

Dorothea would disappear from time to time. I'd go to her room and find out that she'd left, without a forwarding address. It was always the same reason: she hadn't paid the rent for some while. In some cases she'd simply done a bunk during the night.

We always found each other again: or rather, she'd find me, by either turning up at my mother's or by waiting outside the bookshop at closing time.

....

Perhaps love is partly passion and partly compassion, and mostly affection. It isn't just passion, at any rate.

Compassion isn't demeaning. I need compassion, and so does everyone. Or so I believe. It may be a fairly small part of the equation, but still a significant one.

Some people feel they have to humble themselves to accept this. Some are too proud.

Koalas don't feel like this – the ones who are especially wise, that is. Norm taught me this in my dreams. Although admittedly, many koalas quarrel and fight, not showing much compassion or sense of sharing.

But perhaps there is a better term for what I mean, rather than compassion: "loving-kindness," as the Buddhists would put it.

....

The first time I stayed all night with Dorothea, I phoned home to tell my mother I wouldn't be back until the morning, making the excuse that I was staying over with an older male friend she knew by name.

"Hello, it's Denis."

"Denis who?"

"Your son Denis!"

"Oh, Denis, hello!"

I forgave her, because I'd seldom if ever had cause to phone home: up until this time.

When my father died of a heart attack, I became depressed. Bert and I had not been especially close, but I'd still been fond of him, and his dying came as a shock. Also, I was deeply in love with my English teacher, Gay: an adolescent crush, of course, but a serious one. Gay knew that I was interested in writing, so she invited me to her home to meet her husband Leonard, who was a novelist and painter. She meant well, of course, but Leonard and I didn't take to one another, and I became even more smitten – besotted, even – with her. I began to feel hopeless – literally, without any hope. So I tried to kill myself. Needless to say, I was not successful. In the hospital, a doctor tried to convince Mum to have me committed there. She asked me what I wanted, and I replied that I wanted to go home. So she said no to the doctor. I understood then, fully for the first time, that she loved me.

Our Alsatian bitch, Kaya, was waiting for me when I returned from Dorothea's, her nose under the door of my room. She wagged her tail and looked up at me expectantly. I patted her.

....

Dorothea and I began to have dreams about Norm. They post-dated my 'Stigmata' piece, so I don't know why I saw fit to begin with a koala when I wrote it. Through the dreams we slowly pieced together the story of Norm's captivity and escape, his meeting with Aldous and Humbert, and, more sketchily for some reason, his adventures since then.

After a while we started to understand that he was trying to make it to our time, and that we were to meet him.

"Norm's coming," we'd say to each other on waking, or "He'll soon be here."

Why did Norm choose us – if "choose" is indeed the right word? To put it another way: Why did we receive his messages in our dreams?

I suppose it was because we were *receptive*. Dorothea and I never came up with a better explanation.

We never understood how the dreams were transmitted to us, if that is even the way to put it: for perhaps "transmitted" is misleading. We even wondered if Norm himself knew.

Sometimes Dorothea and I would have different dreams about Norm on the same night; at other times one of us would dream about him and the other wouldn't; and very occasionally we'd have the same dream on the same night. Who could explain?

Perhaps it was more that we tapped into *something*, and that something was to do with Norm.

....

I understood that Dorothea slept rough from time to time. In public places: in parks, under bridges, in derelict buildings, even on streets. That's why I left home and rented a room of my own.

5.

Melanie Safka's *Lay Down (Candles in the Rain)* had drawn attention to Meher Baba: numerous people who had never heard of him before were intrigued through her singing.

Zack was delighted.

Baba was the silent guru or spiritual teacher. He'd given up speaking but used an alphabet board or hand gestures to convey his messages and writings. I couldn't see the point. If you were going to be silent, be silent. Or else speak.

He wasn't just a guru. He was, or so it was claimed, the Avatar, the God-man, or, more simply, God.

As with a whole host of other teachings, he invoked the idea of a movement from the One to the Many and back to the One, involving reincarnation, illusion-shedding and God-realization.

His account of all this was highly complicated.

He smiled a great deal. Really, unless you were somehow entranced by a silent, smiling Indian using an alphabet board, I couldn't see the attraction.

At any rate, I can now say that I prefer koala wisdom.

Zack was unwilling to admit that Baba had died. He always said that Baba had "dropped his body," which sounded faintly obscene somehow.

Zack was tall and thin, with dark brown hair, a long face and a Van Dyke beard. He was serious and studious, but also kindly and good-humoured.

Meher Baba wasn't his only interest. Zack had for some time been at work on a book about architecture. His starting point was the simplest interventions in space, whether it was a plank placed against a wall, a roped-off area or electric lights in a tree. These things were not yet architecture, but they pointed towards it, or so he believed: either in terms of structure or embellishment. Caves were also not yet architecture, because there was no or at least little human intervention or creation. After that he looked at the ways in which cliffs or very large trees like the baobab could be hollowed out to live in, or how un-natural objects like boxes could be arranged and adapted as spaces for living, as well as looking at elementary habitation structures like tents and tipis. Enclosure or containment and access or opening-out (or –up) became key terms in this.

The tipi and the standard tent were Zack's fundamental archetypes. "Aspiration" was his key term here. The tipi pointed upwards towards the sky, the tent didn't. Gothic cathedrals embodied aspiration, whereas igloos didn't. Gaudi was his primary example of a modern aspirational architect – and even then it was mainly the Sagrada Família. Skyscrapers were for the most part simply tall buildings, not aspirational ones.

This seemed to me very reductive and prejudiced. The idea of "centering" was in the air – M C Richards' book of that title had come out a few years before – and igloos were surely a model of centredness. And the idea that a Gothic cathedral – any such cathedral – is intrinsically better or more spiritual than a Franciscan chapel – any such chapel – is misguided at best: or so it appeared to me. Humility and grace – receptiveness to the divine – are at least as important as aspiration.

....

I was a bookseller, or, perhaps more accurately, someone who worked for a bookseller. As such... no, more out of my own inclination, I spent many lunch hours and portions of weekends in some of the more curious shops that sold books. I looked amongst the most lively and also some of the worst reading, hoping to come across obscure and even unknown gems – things that had been passed by and warranted discovering. I was as delighted if I found something by Curt Siodmak, the German émigré novelist and scriptwriter working in Hollywood in *film noir* and horror genres, as I'd be to find a book by the excellent and highly unusual poet William Hart-Smith.

....

One day at the shop the conversation turned to the painter Francis Bacon.

"Bacon's an atheist. But you could possibly align his paintings with Tertullian's notion that the saved look down with pleasure on the sufferings of the damned."

I paused.

"Except there are no saved in his world. The pleasure remains, somehow."

"You're reading *Tertullian?*" Zack queried.

"Only dipping in. I'm far more interested in Origen and Clement of Alexandria. But I have to admit I haven't read much of any of the Church Fathers."

"Hmm," said Rollo. "You're not advocating Tertullian, surely?"

"Not that side of him, anyway. But you get something similar in a modern writer like the Anglican novelist Charles Williams, a sort of gloating about the notion of damnation. He's a brilliant writer, but nasty."

I paused.

"I've heard he's a nasty piece of work," I said. "Francis Bacon, that is."

"You know, your face is rather similar to his," Rollo said. "You could be his son – if he was that way inclined."

"Thanks."

....

Rollo made sardonic comments on some of the regular customers. There was an artist whose mixed media works were inspired by mandalas and yantras. "He makes nice fireplaces," Rollo joked. Unfortunately I couldn't look at that man's art without thinking of fireplaces after that. Another regular was involved in the paranormal. "She makes objects move across tables by staring at them: *apparently*." Rollo laughed his dry, self-conscious laugh.

There was also a youngish man who haunted the sheet music section. He'd come into the shop and browse for quite a while, and then buy a single score: always from a selection of Portuguese *fado* songs and music from the 1920s and '30s. Then he'd come back another day and do exactly the same thing. We guessed he didn't have much money. Also there was something glittering and hungry-looking about his gaze, and his manner was curiously furtive. It may sound unkind, but Rollo and I had him pegged as a classic loser. One day he appeared with a sleek young woman, dark-haired and heavily made-up, who wore a fake fur coat and smiled with half-closed eyes in a self-satisfied way. He selected another score. "Kiss me, darling!" he exclaimed to his companion. "My band will play this music and we'll be a big success!" She kissed him – not reluctantly – but in an indifferent and desultory way. Rollo and I looked at each other and nodded.

....

Amongst Rollo's recent works was a series of photographs of a long roll of white linoleum being unrolled and rolled up again on his parents' lawn. A photo was taken at intervals derived by chance.

"Why not use a Persian rug instead?" I asked. "Wouldn't it be more interesting visually?"

Rollo looked at me askance and then snorted.

....

I was doubtful about Conceptual art and didn't mind sharing my doubts with Rollo.

"Even if you accept that concepts alone can constitute art, the art is only as good as the concept – and the concepts usually are extremely impoverished."

"So, do you see any exceptions?"

"Well, Lawrence Weiner – his words seem quite poetic to me, in a very pared-down way, though I know he doesn't see his work that way. Concepts becoming poetry, perhaps? And Roman Opalka, with his painted numbers from nought to infinity...."

"Weiner sees his work as completely unpoetic and as art. His words are art, not poetry," Rollo said.

"He's wrong."

Rollo sniffed.

"And Opalka?"

"He's doing something about time and infinity, and the series can never be completed. In that sense it's a flawed life's work, intentionally so. And it's hand-painted, so it has that about it. Something personal, something slightly crafted: not *purely* conceptual. And crazy: a response to the idea of the complete work that's necessarily going to be incomplete."

"What about Daniel Buren?"

"The stripe guy? No."

"Ed Ruscha?"

"Well, *somewhat* interesting."

"Hmm," said Rollo and then snorted.

Ruscha's work was somewhat similar to Rollo's, in as much as he worked with photographic series – rather plain photographs, deliberately so, of subjects such as gas stations. I guess I'd hit a nerve.

"Chance," I said. "Could it be one factor or element amongst others? Something disruptive? Not the entire thing?"

Rollo snorted.

....

The show of Rollo's I most liked consisted of a large series of photographs of people he passed on his way to work each day, chosen at random by numbers: the first person encountered, then the third, then the fifth, and so on. They were extremely ordinary photos, without fuss or even framing as such; and arranged chronologically in grids, with dates and times. Some people turned up again and again, others only once. Rollo told me he'd asked permission of everyone he'd included: it showed, in the faces and poses; and not at all in a negative way; just, in fact, the opposite. If anyone ever said 'No', he'd simply move on to the next number in the series. Few did, however. He would of course have to improvise a little; while he was photographing Person No. 1, others who might have been Person No. 2 in the series would have gone by; and there was also the problem of groups of people. Ah well: such are the complexities of life and art. Rollo's name for the series was 'People I Passed on My Way to Work.'

....

I suggested to Rollo that he do a series of photos of Martello Towers. But he didn't and wouldn't travel: he seriously wouldn't travel. Sussex was about as far as he would go from his home in North London. He had aunts and uncles scattered around Bognor Regis, Hove, Eastbourne and Hastings, and had become fond of these places from childhood onwards.

6.

Then Dorothea had a breakdown.

The birds and animals spoke to her: sparrows, pigeons, crows, magpies, blackbirds, squirrels, cats, dogs, mice... all of them. Eventually they addressed her by name, she said: and they talked and talked and talked.

7.

(From Dorothea's diary)

"I'm feeling a little... *lost* today," said the pigeon. "I'm not sure what's wrong. I somehow feel... *unfulfilled*... almost *empty*. Oh, I know I'm sounding silly, but even so.... Ah!"

"Perhaps you just need to eat something!" said the crow.

"Yes, some fish!" said the seagull. "But I guess fish is not really for you. Ah well, whatever you can scavenge."

"Is it more to do with the heart?" asked the hedge sparrow, the little dunnock.

"Well, no," said the pigeon. "My wife and I are quite happy, we peck and groom each other affectionately... sweet and gentle pecks, of course!"

"Ah, but the heart may need more!" said the dunnock.

A magpie flew down to the garden and pecked a little amongst the grass. "Am I missing out on something?" she said.

"We were talking about the pigeon's unease," said the dunnock.

Just then the neighbour's cat, Tiddy, appeared, skulking with intent. I shouted to Denis to chase him off.

We loved Tiddy, but still....

I wasn't surprised that I understood what the birds in the tiny garden outside our small ground floor flat said. Why should I be? (Even if Denis didn't hear them: which seemed very strange to me.) After all, Norman the koala had already spoken to us in our dreams.

8.

Dorothea said:

"I dreamt that you and I were in a family gathering, with your mother and your uncle, Frank, and others. A strange, wild girl entered the room; she had a pointed chin, intense eyes and very black hair. 'I love you,' she said to me.

" 'I can't love you', I said honestly. 'I'm not attracted to other women, and besides, Denis is my boyfriend.'

"I would not have said this in front of your mother or uncle, but in the dream I did.

" 'I love you!' she wailed. 'Kiss me!'

"She smashed windows, broke down doors. I saw that more was involved when she suddenly disappeared and just as suddenly reappeared again.

" 'I love you!' she wailed.

"I caught hold of her and kissed her full on the mouth, my tongue seeking hers.

"It was the sweetest kiss.

"We were on a hillside in the country, with livestock around us.

"The demons quit her and fled into the pigs; and they ran off the hill and plunged into the waters below.

"Poor pigs!

"Night had fallen, and the girl was gone: you and I were alone together.

"We kissed. And I awoke. "

9.

(From Dorothea's diary)

And then the animals – cat and dog, mouse and vole, squirrel and fox, and of course hedgehog – also began to speak....

....

Dorothea left off writing at that point; and she never told me more. Except that the birds and the animals spoke *to* her: that is, *they began to address her.*

Finally I persuaded her to admit herself to a psychiatric clinic. I made all the arrangements, and we initially went to see the place and talk to a doctor there.

On the day she was to be admitted we made the journey again by bus, a long way from where we were living. She asked me not to get off at the final stop for her, as she hated goodbyes. "It's not goodbye," I said, and we kissed; then she left the bus and waved to me as she walked away. I stayed on until the next stop and then got off and started back.

I thought I would walk for a while before catching the return bus. I came to a pub and decided to have a drink. My Uncle Frank was in the bar, which came as an enormous surprise, as Frank lived in Somerset, where he grew roses.

"Denis!" he exclaimed. "Imagine coming across you. This is so nice. Let me buy you a drink."

I noticed that he looked as if he'd been crying.

"What brings you here, Uncle Frank? You're a long way from home. Have you been visiting Mum?"

I inwardly apologised to myself for the clichés.

"No, though I should while I'm here. Denis, it's your Aunt Opal: she's terribly ill. The doctors at our local hospital don't know what's wrong, though it's obvious she's failing. They advised me to bring her here to see some specialists. She's having some tests now. It's not the cancer – that's still in remission – but I think that's what's to blame: it's worn her out and made her lose her desire to live."

"Oh God, I'm so sorry, Uncle Frank!"

I'd always liked Frank and Opal: they were good, kind people, down-to-earth, somewhat artless. They had no airs or pretensions. Frank was a large man who'd been a farmer for most of his life; he was on the beefy side, but quite pleasantly so. In contrast, Opal was rather scrawny and frail-looking, even before her illness: I don't say this to be unkind, merely factual.

Frank and I talked for an hour or so, and then I left him and wandered off to catch the bus home. He was quite drunk by then.

10.

The time finally came when we dreamt that Norm was about to appear out of the River of Time. We hurried to Herne Bay and then on to the place of disappearances and reappearances.

"You've come," Norm said, sitting in the boat with us. We'd had to pull him out of the water.

"I don't seem to get any better at swimming," he said, shaking his furry head. "I've almost drowned a number of times. Fortunately there's always a boat around, one way or another."

"How did you know we'd be here on this day and at this time?" Dorothea asked.

"Spirit dreams," Norm replied. "You've been having them, too, haven't you?"

We both nodded.

11.

Should it come as a surprise that it was Rollo who had been so taken with my stories about Norm that when he acquired a holiday home in Felpham, he made sure there was a eucalyptus tree there? It was surprising to me. I guess you never can tell.

He'd achieved some modest fame and fortune by then, partly through his art, partly through writing music criticism for the newspapers.

Rollo had always lived in an Alice in Wonderland sort of world, despite the banality of most of his subject-matter as an artist. I suppose that's why he was prepared to accept Norm's entrance into our existence. Perhaps he wasn't even a *real* materialist: who knows?

He'd taken photographs of the knives, forks and spoons in his kitchen drawer on successive occasions for 2018 nights, for instance. Every time the objects would be in different positions, the colours and shapes of the implements would change according to the arrangement. I can imagine a very young Rollo being fascinated by such things. I think he wanted to recapture that sense of wonder. The entire series was only ever exhibited once, so vast it was.

But more than that, he was either kinder or more empathetic than I'd given him credit for, or his peculiarities just jig-sawed into position with what was happening with us. I suspect the latter: but I could be mistaken.

I can't say I'd thought he ever liked me. Yes, he talked with me, he was sometimes considerate, but he was downright strange and self-absorbed for the most part.

He went through a period of collecting cigarette and cigar packets, studying their designs and trying to work with them. He didn't smoke. (Nor did he drink.) When I told him Dorothea smoked, he kept the cigarettes and cigars and gave them to me to give to her. But when he lost interest in the designs, then that was quite simply the end of that.

12.

So Norm and I were in Felpham, courtesy of Rollo's generosity. Zack had given me indefinite leave from the shop: another unexpected act of generosity. Felpham is a small village near Bognor Regis, in Sussex. We were not involved in a William Blake pilgrimage. But given how small a village Felpham is, it's perhaps not too surprising that Blake's cottage is a strong point of interest, probably more than anything else. There *is* the sea. And we did indeed go down to the beach. The wind blew Norm's ear fur around so much that he begged to be returned to my cloth bag. On the way back to the flat where we were staying, we stopped in front of Blake's cottage. I took Norm out of the bag so that he could see it, but I was a little surreptitious about doing so, as there were *genuine* Blake pilgrims about, and he and I both felt a little embarrassed.

We were not genuine Blake pilgrims, as I've already indicated: hence our embarrassment.

We were there because there was nowhere else to go. I didn't have a eucalyptus tree where I lived, nor was there one at Mum's; or even Uncle Frank's. Norm couldn't live on roses; he couldn't live on anything else than eucalyptus leaves.

Norm and I were feeling sad: very sad indeed. Dorothea had had another breakdown and was in the clinic again. We hated the separation from her. It hurt horribly.

We did find there was good fish and chips in the village, also good Indian food, and good Chinese takeaway. As well as a friendly pub. And of course there was the sea to go down to.

Even so, I woke so many days feeling I would prefer to end my life. Then I'd look at his lovely face and think: well, there are some good things in this world. Also, he seemed to be gazing at me as if to say, "Don't kill yourself, Denis. Who'd look after me? And who'd look out for Dorothea when she comes home?"

Indeed.

And together we survived our time alone in Felpham.

....

This time I insisted on visiting Dorothea in the hospital. I made the journey from Felpham to London as often as I could. At first, my visits were heart-rending, but there was a turn within a few weeks. Dorothea responded very well indeed to the medication she was prescribed. But I knew that I'd have to make sure she kept taking it, once she was released: something I'd not been sufficiently good at before.

....

Grace? Perhaps it's something to do with the Beatitudes.

"Blessed are they who love deeply in abandonment."

....

We'd say to each other, "We should cut down on our drinking."

We said it almost every day.

We never did.

....

Dorothea and I decided to marry.

"We'll have to tell Flora."

"I know," she said.

"And Uncle Frank."

"Oh, that's not a problem, surely?"

"I don't suppose so."

"What about Norm?"

"Well, he wants to go home."

"I know he does. Oh dear."

It occurred to me that many people would consider us – perhaps me especially – as foolish. But sometimes the foolish way is the right way.

....

I was apprehensive when Rollo called to say he was coming down for the weekend. As I keep saying, Rollo was *very* strange. And Dorothea was... Dorothea.

But I was in for a surprise.

"Yes," said Rollo, "she's lovely."

I *was* surprised: she wasn't like his Mayfair women: not at all.

I changed my mind about him.

13.

I decided to splash out on a taxi from the clinic back to our flat.

The taxi-driver was young, friendly and talkative. He seemed Indian, but told us he was Italian. We had to believe him.

When we passed London Zoo, he suddenly said, "Oh, all my life I want to see a koala! I go to Australia to see a koala. That's what I want! My wife, she says no, but I really want to see a koala, and I'll do it someday!"

I didn't say we had a koala at our place. Nor did Dorothea: we looked at each other and nodded.

. . . .

"What we need to do is find a way to take you back to your homeland. But I'm not sure how we're going to do it. I'd have to raise the money for a flight, somehow or other. Even then, I don't know how we'd get you through the security checks."

"I don't know what a security check is, let alone how we'd fly back to Australia. You don't need to go to all that trouble, though. You just have to get me to a place I've heard about... it's in somewhere called Dorset."

"*Dorset?* That's no problem at all. But in what way would it help to go there?"

"Well, you know about the River of Time. There's a place in Dorset where you can find the River of Time and Space. I've been listening out in my travels in time, and I've learned that if you jump into this river and say the right words..."

"An incantation?"

"Yes. If you say the right words, and have what we call a true spirit, you'll come out of the water in the place and time you want to be."

"That's utterly extraordinary! Are you sure about this, though? It's not just a story – a myth?"

"It's a real story; a true myth."

"Could we come as well?" Dorothea asked.

Norm shook his head.

"You could never get back again," he said. "I wouldn't advise it."

"All right," I said, "but we need to know whereabouts in Dorset this river is. Dorset's a very big place."

"If you can get me to somewhere called Way Mouth, I'll know what to do from there."

"Ah! Weymouth."

"Yes, Way Mouth."

......

Norm later expanded upon this matter of The River of Time and Space.

"I'd pieced it all together the last time I entered this place through The

River of Time, but I didn't know anyone who would help me get to where I needed to be. To Way Mouth, I mean. And though I travelled a good deal by myself in the bush lands, it's not at all easy for me here. Not at all."

He paused.

"It was Humbert's son who'd worked it out."

"You don't mean Humbert J Brockenhurst?" I asked, incredulous. Of course I knew about Norm's talks with Aldous and Humbert in the 1920s.

"Humbert eventually became obsessed with my story, much against his will," continued Norm. "You see, I'd sent him a dream, just as I once said I would. I won't try to tell you what it was, but it convinced Humbert. He filled his son's ears with details of my story; he even named him Hubert N Brockenhurst. You can guess what the 'N' stands for." He looked amused, as amused as a koala can look. "Hubert guessed that there must also be a River of Time and Space, if there's a River of Time. He devoted years and years to testing river water, beginning with The River of Time, and travelling around the country and listening to stories that had to do with strange comings and goings related to water. He also spent a great deal of time in his father's vast library, going over spells and magic chants and so on. He wrote papers, which were dismissed by almost everyone. He also published accounts of his experiments with The River of Time and Space, with the same result."

He paused.

"I need to take a nap," he said.

14.

The next day Norm resumed his account.

"I found out where he was and went to see him. He'd been living for some time in Herne Bay, not very far from The River of Time and the compound where we exiled koalas were kept captive. He was surprised to meet me – more than surprised – shocked and also overjoyed. He brought out some wine for himself and bottled water for me, and we kept toasting each other. He became what you call 'drunk,' and more and more friendly, as well as boastful. I saw my chance. I told him I didn't believe anything he said. He looked hurt and indignant, and told me all sorts of details, including the words to say for getting back to my homeland."

Dorothea lit a cigarette. "Didn't he give you the formula – the words – for getting back again?" she asked.

"I never asked."

"You don't just think he was – ?" I was going to say "mad." "Deluded?"

"Oh, everything he said made sense. Also, we'd been getting on very well, especially before I told him I didn't believe him. But then he tried to capture me. I had to climb out a window and down some sort of pipe and then scamper into the bushes. I've become really good at making escapes over the years."

......

During one conversation Norm mentioned some things being true and others not.

"True – ", I said.

"Rather than false?" said Dorothea,

"But – ", I said.

"It's just like wisdom. Seeing into the very heart of things: as Aldous once put it in a dream I had; I owe that to him, if nothing else."

....

"Koala wisdom might be a sort of illness…," Dorothea suggested.

"No," I said. "No."

"I didn't mean it as something bad," she said.

"I know you didn't," said Norm. "But I really don't think so."

15.

We boarded a train at Waterloo a few days later, bound for Weymouth: Norman, Dorothea and I.

Norm spent most of the journey in my cloth bag, to avoid unwanted curiosity. I managed to arrange things so that he could just peep out, with the bag facing a window and one side of it – the one nearest the window – pulled down a little. In any event, he slept for much of the way.

It was only when we'd left Dorchester South and the carriage had otherwise emptied that I took him out of the bag. He gazed avidly at the passing scenery. However, I suspect he was thinking of his homeland, his beloved bush, and how different it was: and how good it would be to see it again.

....

Dorothea and I took turns cuddling Norm and saying goodbye. I put him down and he scampered to the edge of the river. He looked back and nodded to us.

I called out to him: "Have you said the magic words? To yourself?"

"No," said Norm. "I've realised I only need to believe in the Great Spirit Koala and be a true spirit."

He paused.

"It's koala wisdom. I was misled for a while."

He paused again, as if pondering what else to say – what *final* thing.

"Koala wisdom can never die. It can only be returned to the Great Spirit Koala."

Then he dove into the water and disappeared from sight.

We were both pleased for him: we'd wanted him to be happy, and we'd planned for this very event. But all the same, as we stood on the shore we wept: wept uncontrollably... inconsolably.

"Norm should have been at our wedding!" Dorothea cried. "Why didn't we ask him to wait?"

"I know!" I sobbed. "I know!"

Epilogue

This is what I've since gleaned from spirit dreams.

Dorothea and I will die at roughly the same time. From the way we look in the dreams, this will probably be in ten years or so.

It happens differently from dream to dream, though with numerous recurrences: there is still a play of possibilities, because these events haven't happened yet. Why some features are constant rather than others, I can't say.

One possibility is that we both die of cirrhosis of the liver. It would be fitting. Dorothea is older and has been drinking heavily for longer, but you can never tell about these things. At any rate, one of the few constants is that we die together, give or take some minutes or possibly a few hours.

Another possibility is that we die in a car crash. There's a drunken driver, whose face I can never see clearly; neither can Dorothea. It's never one of us driving: for neither of us drive.

There are other scenarios. None are any more savoury or instructive, I have to admit.

Dorothea has of course had the same or similar dreams. She's resigned. I suppose I am, too.

The end of each dream is always the same.

I seem to awake (or rather, we seem to awake – but let me tell it from my point of view). I'm in a warm, sunny place with grass and trees and a blue sky. I can't see any sun, but the light is wonderfully clear. Yes, so far so banal, you could say. Except that it doesn't *feel* banal: it feels natural and yet extraordinary at the same time. And then I see Dorothea. I recognise her instantly, even though she's walking on all fours and is covered in brown and white fur; she has large furry ears and a large black nose. She's simply beautiful... *so* beautiful. She raises her eyes and the eyes widen, and she smiles – as far as a koala can be said to smile. I look down at myself. I'm on all fours and I'm covered in fur, too.

Someone else approaches, also a koala. I recognise him immediately.

"You've come," Norm says.

Messages for Dominic

Enter Iredell

A koala carrying a miniature didgeridoo stopped another koala, also carrying a tiny didgeridoo.

"Aw, could you give me a sound on your didg, mate?"

"Yeah, 'course I can."

And he did.

The first koala then sounded his own instrument, until the two didgeridoos were in tune.

"Aw, thanks, mate."

"No problems."

And they went on their separate ways.

But suddenly the first koala stopped and turned, as if facing me.

"This isn't really your dream, mate," he said; "it's mine."

I woke then, utterly bemused and bewildered.

I looked at the alarm clock; barely half an hour before I'd have to get up and ready myself for the journey to work. "Dominic, Dominic," I addressed myself and sighed. I switched the alarm off and went back to sleep.

....

A koala was swimming across a river: I recognised him as the same furry creature from my dream of two nights ago, the one who'd seemed to be speaking to me. And I was there too, in a skiff. He stopped swimming and began to sink, but not before he was within reach. I scooped him up from the water and put him down in the boat.

"Aw, thanks, mate," he said.

He caught his breath, looking around him and clearly thinking about things – he had that look.

My alarm clock sounded: time to get up for work again.

....

On the way home from work I got caught in a thunderstorm, and I was only in a T-shirt, thin slacks and sandals, and without an umbrella. So I ducked into a pub not far from St Pancras Station: it looked friendly enough, but how wrong I was.

I ordered a white wine and found a place to sit.

A man at the table next to mine was saying: "The dead guy, he's that scumbag bibliographer. Bullet in the head. Somebody taking care of business."

He suddenly gave me what I thought was a meaningful look, although he couldn't possibly know that I'd compiled a bibliography of 1960s UK poetry books.

I turned away and put my head down, opening a book of poetry.

"He's reading a book!" a drunken woman sitting at the bar bellowed. "Look at him!"

I tried to ignore her.

"*A book!* Look at the bugger! He's *reading! He's reading a book!*"

The time-honoured phrase, "what have I done to deserve this?", occurred to me.

Another drunk chimed in: "I read a book once." He paused. "It just made me unhappy."

My God, I thought, I prefer having dreams about talking koalas!

......

I may have engaged in research to my liking, courtesy of a grant, and I may have done – and continue to do – other research, not always so tuned to my interests (and sometimes utterly unrelated to them), but that's my living. What do I do otherwise and for myself? I write. I'm a writer.

Who are my literary influences? A somewhat motley crew: William Saroyan, Paul Goodman, Cyril Connolly, Stefan Themerson, Miguel de Unamuno, Henri Michaux.... I suppose that list of names would only make sense to me: I mean, the confluence makes sense in my own writing but probably in no other way.

Have I said that I knew Themerson a little? Who wouldn't like a novella with a title like 'Wooff Wooff or Who Killed Richard Wagner?' How could I resist writing to him and sending him something of my own?

He phoned me some weeks later and said, "My wife and I would like to meet you. Could you come to our place for dinner tomorrow night?"

I could and did.

Stefan and his wife Franciszka were in their 60s; he was a poet and philosopher as well as a fiction writer, and she was a painter and graphic artist. They'd escaped from the Nazis in the early 1940s, finding ways of getting themselves out of France, where they'd been living, and then settling in England. He was not very talkative, but clearly (I thought) wise; she was loquacious and acute. They both struck me as kindly and generous souls.

After the meal, Stefan smoked his pipe and we all drank vodka.

"Well, we've read your story, or what there is of it. When do you think you'll finish it?" He paused. "You know we run our own small press? We might be able to publish your story."

Needless to say I've never finished it. It's called 'The Wrong Artist.' It's about a painter named Harry Graham, but a hedgehog also plays a part in it.

My trouble, you see, is that I can start a story, and I can even sometimes write its ending, but I can't seem to ever end up with a complete piece.

Then there's the story about sloths, 'No Hurry.' I haven't even started that yet.

. . . .

When I'm not writing, I'm working, as I said. Do I take days off at all often from my job? Yes.

I have to phone up and ask for the Head's secretary, a formidable woman to say the least. "Hello," I say, "it's Dominic. I'm afraid I won't be in today, as I'm feeling ill." A frosty silence – *arctic* might be more accurate – ensues. "I see," she finally says. My God, I hate those occasions. But it doesn't put me off calling in sick.

Why? I hate my job. It's boring: the subject of the research – a journalist and broadcaster– isn't even vaguely interesting to someone with my own particular research interests. And I'm tied up in bureaucratic rigmarole; and I have to take orders from people I don't really respect, who are less published, some of them less educated and, to be arrogant, perhaps, less intelligent: no, no, that wouldn't be bad, necessarily, but, rather, *pushed around* by them. I have thought about it as a lesson in humility, but it still sticks in my craw; I know I shouldn't be like this – I chose this way of life, ignoring all ideas of a career and any sort of advancement – and I don't dislike all the people involved. *Some I do*: and I'm thinking now of past jobs I've had as well: fools, bullies, as well as those who give themselves airs without any justification, and uptight and thoroughly tiresome pedants, O, and many more.... And I know I sometimes overreact when I shouldn't really react at all. Ah, well....

Perhaps I'm just not a very nice guy; although I'd like to be.

And here I am now, spending my nights conversing with Iredell....

....

Let's get back to my stories.

There's 'Dorothy and Bonnie: A Story of Two Sisters,' where I imagine the writer Dorothy Parker and the gangster Bonnie Parker are, well, *sisters*. There is no factual support for this, of course, and DP was some seventeen years older than BP (though she outlived her by many years), and the only connection is that they both wrote poetry. (Bonnie's poems were not exactly literary masterpieces, to say the least.) I haven't done anything with this idea so far.

And there's 'When Christmas Came to Ruth,' which concerns the English

Buddhist and High Court Judge Christmas Humphreys, who pronounced sentence on Ruth Ellis, the last woman to be hanged in England. I've got as far as Ellis – who shot her lover dead while arguably in a disturbed state of mind – saying to Humphreys when he visits her in her cell, "You've pronounced me dead while still alive," and Humphreys replying "And are you not?" Purely fictional, of course, and quite possibly unfair to Humphreys: it's just how I imagine such an encounter.

And then there's 'The Suicide Club,' about a literary society whose members hero-worship Sylvia Plath, Anne Sexton, John Berryman, Ann Quin, B S Johnson, Alejandra Pizarnik, Paul Celan and Veronica Forrest-Thomson and wish to emulate them. (*Did* Veronica Forrest-Thomson really commit suicide, or was it an accident? I guess the jury's still out on that one.) As the list might suggest, it's correspondingly a curiously women-dominated society, with a smattering of men. I have no explanations for this, even though I thought the idea up: tougher situations for some of the writers, sure, but surely not for all of them (Anne Sexton, for example)? Yes, OK, and put Papa Ernest Hemingway in there, as someone else to emulate, for one? He doesn't quite fit, somehow: wrong sensibility, perhaps? And perhaps there just haven't been quite such a number of talented literary suicides who were male? And this is just to repeat the question! But going back a bit, there's Georg Trakl, Attila József, Ernst Toller, Stefan Zweig and Walter Benjamin... and then of course, to add to the women, Virginia Woolf. Most of these deaths, however, were strongly related to what was happening in either the First or Second World War. That makes some sort of difference.

'The Apocalypse / The Rapture / The Singularity': a three-layered piece about people who either hate other humans or hate the entire human race so much that they want to see them or it destroyed. I sympathise to some extent, but the scenarios proffered are more depressing than I can deal with. So much so that I can't bear to write the story at all: at least for now.

The one I've done most with so far – and it's not a lot – is 'The Visitor.' It's mainly just a pile of notes, in fact, though I have written a little of the story. But let's come back to that in a bit.

....

I've also toyed with the idea of writing a manual of "creative writing," as it's called, inspired by existing manuals but with a difference. It would be called *A Guide to Creative Writing Heresies, With Practical Advice to the Writing Novice*. (Well, some are more heretical than others, I admit.) Here are the titles of the first few chapters:

1. Tell, Don't Show

2. Hurrah for Long Sentences

3. "Is" and "Was" Unbound

4. Forget Narrative Arcs (and Other Notions Leading to Predictability)

5. The Unities: How to Subvert Them and Why

6. Tips on Successful Information Dumping

7. "I'm So Clever, O So Clever": and How to Sensibly Circumvent Such Idiocy

8. Losing Your Own Voice and Finding Yourself as a Writer

9. Genres: Hybridity and Its Virtues

I would of course give examples, at least for (1)-(9), though with more emphasis on some of these things than others.

For example, (1): have a look at the first sentences of various noteworthy novels, such as Charles Dickens' *A Tale of Two Cities*, where we're told it was the best of times and the worst of times (however much subject to parody this has become), Melville's *Moby Dick*, where the narrator/protagonist tells us to call him Ishmael, Ford Madox Ford's *The Good Soldier*, where the narrator tells us it's the saddest story he's ever heard, Ruth Rendell's *A Judgement in Stone*, where we're told that Eunice Parchman murdered the Coverdale family because she was illiterate. And then there's F Scott Fitzgerald's *The Last Tycoon*, George Meredith's *The Egoist*, George du Maurier's *Peter Ibbetson*... and so on.... Oh, for (2), start off with William Faulkner's best novels and John Donne's prose. For (3), to combat the weird hostility to the use of "is" and "was", have a look at James Agee's *Let's Us Praise Famous Men*. And, yes, let's skip to (6): oh gosh, how about Mrs Gaskell's *Mary Barton* for an example? Or for that matter the 'Cetology' chapter of *Moby Dick*? I admit (5) may seem an odd choice – why should anyone still worry about Aristotle's "unities," especially if they're not writing drama? Possibly because the "unities" are easy to teach, making things seem simple?

That's as far as I've got.

......

So why am I dreaming about koalas?

If you've read this far, you'll know that I think and write about animals – sloths, hedgehogs, and so on. And the animals do speak.

......

"Do you have a name?" I asked the koala when I next dreamt of him.

He looked like he was frowning, as far as a koala could be said to.

"'Course I do, mate. It's Iredell."

"What sort of a name for a koala is *Iredell*?"

"What sort of a name is Dominic?"

"There's nothing wrong with my name!"

"Nothing wrong with mine, either, Dom," he responded.

"No one calls me *Dom*!"

"Someone does now, mate."

He paused.

"Anyway, Dom, it's like this: I need your help. I'm stuck in a place called Herne Bay."

"That shouldn't be a problem. I could come and get you. Herne Bay's not that far from London."

"Yeah, but here it's 1801 or 1802 or something like that. What year is it there?"

"It's 1978."

"See what I mean?"

Iredell paused.

"I know that other koalas have done it," he finally said.

"Sorry, done what?"

"You know, got out of Herne Bay in 1802 or whatever year it is."

"How do you know?"

"I've had spirit dreams about them."

"*Spirit dreams*?" I queried.

"Yeah, they're special dreams that reveal something important to you. Koalas have them a lot. It's just how we are!"

"But how did you come to be in Herne Bay?" I asked.

"I was brought here from Australia," said Iredell. "As a convict."

"As a *what*?!"

"You heard me, mate. There was a colony of us – a penal colony. We were supposed to be producing eucalyptus oil."

"You were supposed to be doing *what*?!"

"Please stop doing that, mate."

"Doing *what*?"

Iredell sighed, or appeared to. He clearly decided to ignore my interruptions and just get on with his story.

"There was a mad businessman, who managed to find backers for this scheme of his. Because koalas live off eucalyptus leaves, he thought he could find a way of getting us to help extract oil from the leaves. He was as convincing as he was bonkers, I guess. So we got rounded up and put in a ship.... It was horrible, mate. Many of us died, and those who survived were little better than dead."

His voice choked and tears began to fall down his furry cheeks. I was sorry for him.

"We had a Koala Elder with us," he continued. "Norman, his name was. And please don't say that's an odd name for a koala! He was really wise. A bit of a tub-thumper, though."

He paused, sniffling a little.

"There was also someone named David, quite a nice guy...."

He cocked his head and looked searchingly at me.

"You remind me a little of him, mate," he finally said. "But of course he was better looking... and smarter."

"Gee, thanks!"

"It's still no small compliment, mate. David was the first of us to escape the compound."

"And you escaped afterwards?"

"Yeah, right after: we knew we had to. That mad scheme about eucalyptus oil hadn't worked, and they were talking about selling us off for some sort of medical experiments." He involuntarily shuddered.

I did as well. "Ghastly!"

"You said it, mate."

"So what happened?"

"I ran and hid, ran and hid, but eventually I went back to the compound one night: I had to, I was starving! It seemed to be deserted, so I fed and then ran and hid again. I've been doing the same thing for some time now. The place still seems deserted, but they might come back."

"So basically you're still in hiding?"

"That's it, mate! And eventually someone *will* come there! *I need help!*"

It was admittedly a rather long dream.

And these dreams really weren't like ordinary dreams: they were more coherent for the most part, without the slipping and sliding from one thing or person or scene to another, the ambiguities....

But were they *spirit dreams?*

Ray, Isabelle and Hope

A shabby-looking man in dirty sweater and jeans tried to pick my pocket by embracing me at the bus-stop: "Let me give you a hug," he said after initiating a few minutes of conversation. And he hugged me again on the bus. I kept my coat tight against me, shielding my trouser pockets.

Nice try, I thought, but no luck, buddy.

Why I try to sound like a tough guy in my thoughts, I've no idea: I'm anything *but*.

However, the encounter made me think of Ray, for the first time in a while.

....

I was living in a suburb of London called Notting Hill. It was my habit to take long walks at night, through the poorer parts of the neighbourhood into the more affluent and back again. It was on one of these walks, and in a poorer area, that I encountered Ray.

As I was walking along, someone crossed over the road and fell in step with me, as if it was the most natural thing to do.

He was short, slight, clean-shaven and prematurely balding – I'd have guessed he was in his thirties. "Hello," he said, "I'm Ray."

"I'm Dominic."

He smiled. "I've only just got out of prison. I don't know anyone around here. I'm staying in a half-way house."

"Why were you in prison?"

"I'm a thief."

I was a little thrown, but he seemed such a friendly person.

"I'm a writer," I said. "I write stories."

Ray smiled. "If I were a writer, I'd probably use a Hermes typewriter – maybe a Hermes Baby."

I laughed. "I get the joke," I said.

"How about a drink?" he suggested.

"Sure," I said.

....

So Ray and I bumped into each other on a couple of other occasions, enjoyed talking to each other, and ended up becoming friends. Ray would come by my place and say, "Would you like to go for a walk?"

Ray's idea of a walk meant trotting off to the nearest pub.

I didn't mind in the least.

....

I remember Ray turning up at my door just as I was saying goodbye to a fellow doctoral student, Douglas. He'd called by supposedly to discuss the latest chapter of my bibliographic thesis, but really just wanted to get some advice on his own. I introduced them to each other, and we all talked for a while before Douglas said he really had to go.

"He seems like a nice guy," Ray said when Douglas was at some distance down the street.

"He's a shit," I said.

"Really?"

"Well, maybe a nice shit."

"Isn't that a contradiction in terms?" asked Ray. "Like a round square?"

"Or a Christian atheist?"

We both laughed.

"Oh yes," Ray said, "that's just ethical humanism in Biblical fancy dress!"

"Except that Christian atheists usually try to look and sound as modern as possible!"

"By the way, is there any sign of rain?"

"No."

"The wind's at work, though."

"Certainly is."

Ray paused.

"So what would a nice shit be like?"

"Douglas."

"Oh, come on, Dominic...."

"Someone who climbs up ladders, either socially or to do with careers or both; someone who acts like a friend, really seems a friend, until you're of no use anymore, even something of an embarrassment, given their new status.... They may remain somewhat friendly, or they may not, but they're no longer your friend." I paused. "I've never had a ladder to climb up, nor have I wanted to."

"Nor I!"

He paused.

"But I don't think you should call him a 'shit'."

"Nor do I, really."

I realised I'd been sliding into my tough guy manner.

....

I had a dream about Douglas: that he would become ill, very ill, and then he would recover. And that the illness would save him, so to speak. Illness sours some, leaves others untouched, and wakes others up.

I haven't any idea if this is what happened to Douglas or not. We completely lost touch.

....

I was walking around the back streets of Notting Hill with Ray one night, when we encountered a woman pushing a man in a wheelchair; she immediately began to talk to us ("Do you two live around here?"), and so we fell in together on our stroll.

Isabelle, who introduced herself to us while neglecting to mention the man's name, looked to be in her early forties; she was slender and tall with a tendency to stoop, and she had dark hair and a somewhat long, thin face. She was obviously drunk, and so was her companion. I don't know why, but I thought she had the most debauched and cruel features I'd ever seen: this seemed especially evident in her eyes and mouth; and at the same time she was sexually attractive in the extreme. I couldn't help but feel fascinated: it was obvious to me that I was going to find a way of getting to know her.

Isabelle's clothes – dress and top – and shoes, all dark in colour, were shabby but had probably been stylish and even expensive once. She clutched a pack of cigarettes and a box of matches with one hand while still managing to wheel the chair.

The man's wheelchair had definitely seen better days, but so had he. His lower face was lined with stubble and his eyes bleary; his clothes were close to being rags.

"Cover yourself up!" Isabelle abruptly chided him. "What if there were children around?"

And indeed his fly was open and his cock visible, though I hadn't noticed before.

"I'm something of a cripple myself," she said enigmatically as we parted company, Ray and I heading off towards my flat and his shelter, and she and her companion in the opposite direction.

"What do you think she meant by that?" I asked Ray.

"I have no idea," he replied.

....

Her cruelty was psychological and emotional rather than physical, and she found all sorts of ways to inflict pain.

I suppose I was an obvious target. There are many things about me, I have to admit, that can be laughed at, from my physical and sexual shyness – I don't even like to get undressed in front of someone else – to what she saw as my literary "pretensions."

....

Max the Magician turned up unexpectedly. He was thirteen, and should really have been with one or other of his parents. Or am I old fashioned? Admittedly he only lived across the street.

Max identified with magic, and a good magician he was, indeed: hence his nickname. Though Isabelle's nephew, he had a far more respectable upbringing and home than you might otherwise expect.

"Hello, Isabelle, hello, Dominic!" he called out. He'd become used to me. "Would you like to see a new card trick?"

"Sure," I said.

....

Max the Magician was short, slim, brown-haired and myopic: he looked confident and puzzled at the same time, oddly enough. But then he was only thirteen years old, as I've said.

I recognised in Max's magic tricks some of the elements or characteristics of Ray's thievery, as he'd once obligingly demonstrated to me: sleight-of-hand, misdirection, and sheer speed and dexterity of hands and digits. But young Max only sought to entertain, whereas Ray brought loss to others.

Ray always said he stole solely for profit and to avoid working. When he talked about his acts of theft, however, as he occasionally did, there seemed a pride in his ingenuity and ability to outwit that bordered on arrogance (but who am I to point the finger there?). I wondered about this, especially as that wasn't at all how he usually appeared, and hoped he wouldn't feel compelled to always be a thief, and would gravitate to something... *better*: more in line with his better qualities, I mean. I guess I am a bit of a moralising bugger.

I had no fears about Max ending up like Ray. For one thing, I'd introduced him to the character of Mandrake the Magician: what better role model could he have, with his interests? He might have found Mandrake clichéd, which wouldn't have been too surprising given the distance in time from when the comic strip series began, but he didn't: the suave, well-groomed, elegant and gentlemanly magician in the top hat, tuxedo and cape, who fights against wrong-doers using powers of hypnotism and illusionism that blur into the supernatural, appealed to him just as I'd hoped. Mandrake, although aloof for the most part, can also be surprisingly approachable and even affable. He also has a great girlfriend: nice not to have to make any qualifications for once. "Wow!" Max said. "Cool!" Indeed.

Change a woman into a panther and back again when it benefits both her and the magician himself? Make someone invisible at your command? And much, much else, indeed.... I won't say anything about it being a comic strip, just as I didn't to Max. Nor that I'm basically opposed to the occult, especially when it plays into power. Enough! As a temporary role model for Max, with his interest in magic, Mandrake still seemed a good choice.

....

Why would I want to concern myself with the occult? It's most often about resonances and residues of the physical and psychological: if indeed anything else than what's in people's minds: however powerful. Nothing to do with the spiritual, I'd vouchsafe: at any rate, definitely not when it's to do with power, and at a more strictly personal level, domination and subjugation, authority and self-glorification. And Mandrake? A magician: he plays with people's minds, but sometimes he does seem to cross over into some other territory, even if he employs his various skills for ends that are not at all power-driven, let alone -crazed: unlike my fictional character Harry Graham.

Think of haunted houses: objects levitating, and smashing against walls; and blood running down walls? If such spirits that would do these things exist, don't they have better things to do with themselves?

And people who do get involved in this? It's usually to do with something inane or nasty... or both.

....

When I say Max "identified with magic," I obviously don't mean in the sense of my character Harry Graham.

His story is entitled 'The Wrong Artist,' as I've said. (It's the story, or rather the fragments of a story, that I sent the Themersons.) He practises what might be called theurgic art: an art that magically causes things to happen. He could paint a portrait of someone, and that someone would have to die if they saw the painting, or in another case fall violently in love with the artist, depending on what Harry wished. The paintings would have strange effects on other people who viewed them – individuals other than the subjects, that is – but of a lesser and less specific intensity. It was to do with power and control, in other words. It all began for Harry when he drew a picture of a friend's wife, someone Harry desired. It wasn't a drawing like you or I would make: or if you, definitely not me. Symbols were involved; and odd details such as additional eyes.... He made use of rituals, too, during the making of the picture. And the portrait was indeed effective. And how did Harry treat the woman in question, his friend's wife? He slept with her, of course. Otherwise he treated her contemptuously and cruelly.

How does this story end? Harry wakes one morning and finds himself in a chamber, an all-glass room. A hedgehog is sitting looking at him, not just looking in his direction, but staring up into his eyes. It suddenly picks up a tiny mirror in its front paws and angles it up for Harry to see himself. "You're a hyena!" the hedgehog exclaims. Harry leans forward and peers into the mirror, and sees that he is exactly that. "So I'm a jackal," he says, "I'm Anubis, worshipped by the ancient Egyptians..." "No," cries the hedgehog, "you're not a god! You're not even a jackal, for that matter, you're a hyena, a filthy scavenger!" "But I've painted great paintings! *Powerful* paintings!" The hedgehog says nothing in reply, which enrages Harry. "All right," he says, "if I'm really a hyena, I'll eat you!" But the hedgehog dissolves, mist-like, before him. Harry lunges forward anyway, and hits himself against one of the glass walls. He tries again, and again. Bloodied, he sees that he is completely alone. And in a sudden moment of insight, knows that it's forever. "It's a dream," Harry says to himself in order not to panic. "Just a bad dream!"

Or is it?

. . . .

So if Harry Graham is "the wrong artist," what would "the right artist" be like? I'll have to think about that!

. . . .

And in another version Harry Graham tries to mate with a shark, but the shark eats him. Well, what would you do if you were a shark? Yes, I'd been reading Lautréamont's *Maldoror*: hard not to send up something like that.

. . . .

How did the relationship with Isabelle end? It was after a Christmas Eve party she took me to, at Max's parents'. Max wanted to give us a demonstration of fire-eating, which he'd heard about in connection with a neighbour, a writer, actor and amateur magician named Heathcote. (I'd heard a story about Heathcote trying out this act to impress a girlfriend: it backfired – no pun intended – in that he accidentally set fire to his own hair, which didn't impress the girlfriend at all. But that was some years ago, admittedly: no doubt he'd improved his skills since then.) Max's parents weren't at all keen on the idea, especially as he hadn't had any lessons, so we were treated to the inevitable card tricks instead. I have to confess that I did get extremely drunk at the party, but so of course did Isabelle.

"I don't want to sleep with you tonight!" she said. "You're fat! And pimply! And drunk!" She didn't mince words.

Not that I'd changed shape since she'd last seen me, nor that my skin was really any worse than usual.

The following day she told me I was a pathetic loser and a drunken degenerate and that she was breaking up with me. Yes, it was Christmas Day: a nice time to break up with someone. Too bad, buster, I said to myself. I should have said something about pots and kettles, I suppose.

....

"I wouldn't say you're a degenerate!" said Ray.

"Gee, thanks," I said.

"I think you should make better choices in your girlfriends."

Ray knew a thing or two, I have to admit.

For example, he once said, apropos of a friend of mine he'd been introduced to:

"I don't trust people who refer to themselves as 'seekers,' Dominic. They try things out, they have a taste of this and a taste of that, they're never satisfied because they're still seeking, and that means they don't want to *find*, they just want to *seek*, and if they ever do settle for anything, it will almost inevitably be the worst possible choice, presumably as that's what they've *really* been after."

"That was rather vehement," I said.

He sighed. "It's because my mum and dad were 'seekers.' Mum eventually became a member of one of the Gurdjieff/Ouspensky groups, and Dad joined the Seventh Day Adventists. They divorced, of course. And neither of them speaks to me. Do you see what I mean, Dominic?"

"I agree!" I said. "But how... what...? How have you escaped from this? What have *you* done?"

"Besides stealing?" he asked.

"Oh, come on...."

"I'm Hermes, remember."

"I wish you'd stop stealing and concentrate on the other aspects of being Hermes! Apart from anything else, you'll end up back in prison."

"But I'd have to work for a living!"

"Yes, there is that...," I sighed. I'd never enjoyed any of the jobs I'd had: clerk, cleaner, library assistant, bookseller... I even worked in a toy factory for a while....

"And which other aspects are you thinking of? Do you think I should play tricks on people?"

"No, no..."

"Carry messages?"

"That sounds better."

"You want me to get a job as a *postman*?"

"Well, perhaps...."

"You know, a friend of mine was arrested for being drunk in charge of a milk float."

I laughed.

"Let's go for a drink," he said.

....

I don't think Hope was "the right artist," though I might be wrong.

There was a Swedenborgian Church in Notting Hill. I was curious. I went to a service.

"After we've died, we'll be angels," an elderly black woman told me. Others nodded assent.

...where it is said 'spirits', I'd read, *it meant people in the world of spirits, while 'angels' meant people in heaven.*

I was still considering the distinction....

"Are you a Swedenborgian?" a young, petite, fair-haired woman asked me. She had a friendly mien, as well as an attractive face: but there was also a severity there, and intensity in the eyes. I should have paid more attention to those features, I know now.

She was an artist, as it turned out. Her work was calligraphic, a little along Lettrist lines, perhaps, though she didn't seem aware of this: letters, lines, squiggles, swirls and so forth, all mixed together. The letters didn't make words, and when they looked like they might, squiggles and swirls and even knife cuts put pay to that. She painted on sheets of hard plastic, on glass, on wood and even on metal.

It was.... *interesting*, one might say.

We went out as a couple for a while. It was difficult. She would get into rages for no apparent reason.

"A spirit is a spirit and an angel is an angel," she said. "A spirit could inhabit Hell, but an angel could only inhabit Heaven. I think when you die you might be a spirit but not an angel!"

"Ah!" I said. Was that even worse than what Isabelle said about me? Oh yes. But I tried to weather the maelstrom.

Ray and I were still friends, and I was going to Greece, to see an American poet who lived there. Hope declined to come along with me to Greece, or even to the airport. Ray helped me with my bags. But when we got to the airport and found where we had to be, Hope was waiting there.

"I should leave you two alone," said Ray, and skedaddled.

Hope and I had our usual intense confrontation – what went for a discussion in her terms – although for once there was no shouting. She stared at me.... *intensely*, and then left.

When I saw Ray after eventually returning home, I thanked him for being so sensitive.

"I wasn't being *sensitive*," said Ray; "she scared the shit out of me!"

As you might imagine, the relationship with Hope didn't last. A person who would scratch her own eyes out in her art school graduation photo wasn't going to be the most stable of girlfriends.

She threw coffee in my face in a café in Islington.... or was it Camden

Town? Fortunately the coffee wasn't boiling hot, though it was *somewhat* hot. Goodbye, Hope.

I don't blame the Swedenborgians. She could have been a Christadelphian or Christian Scientist, or Catholic.... or atheist, for that matter. Hope was simply warped. Simply? Well, she was warped, anyway.

Iredell and Cynthia

Ah! Now, I did say I was going to tell you about 'The Visitor'? Can it wait a little longer?

No?

All right, here's the beginning of 'The Visitor':

Benny was taking a night-stroll around the square, in the company of two young men he'd met on the bus from London. As they passed the entrance to their hotel, the desk porter called out: "Is one of you Mr Silverstein?" When Benny affirmed that he was, the porter said, "There's a telephone call for you."

"Happy birthday!" said the voice that came from the receiver, and Benny knew it was his friend Petros.

"It's great to hear your voice," said Benny. "I see you got my card...."

"Sure," said Petros. "Are you still taking the boat tomorrow?"

"Yes, if that's OK?"

"It'll be fine, Benny. I'll see you then."

.

He walked around the streets by himself, after his companions had gone back to the hotel to get some sleep. At one street corner a blind man, with a huge frame, a large, fat, unshaven face and eyes fixed upwards, was playing the piano accordion with virtuoso agility, the music smashing forth upon the air in its jazzy rhythms at breakneck speed. Benny disliked the accordion as an instrument, but he had to admire the man's musicianship. He was even tempted to go to his hotel room and unpack his clarinet, then come back and join in.

He'd not told anyone on the journey about his birthday. But he had let Petros know that he was arriving on the day he turned twenty-two; and so to have had Petros as the sole wisher of his happiness for that day was, he felt, better than to have heard the same or similar words from any number of casual acquaintances.

Tomorrow, he thought, I'll walk to the top of the hill and look out over the city; then I'll catch a train to the port....

You're later introduced to Homer:

"My name is Homer. I'm blind yet far seeing.

"I have heard Petros speak of the visitor, the one named Benny. But then Petros has many visitors: many who come seeking him. He speaks of some, and of those I remember a few."

Petros is a poet, and comes from America, despite the name (which was really given to him by his Greek friends and neighbours). Homer again:

"Petros," Homer said, "is saying what he has to say, and what we need to hear." He didn't say read, *for obvious reasons.*

And Homer again, on Benny:

"How did I know who it was, considering that I'm blind? His voice, of course, the

same as I recognise Petros' voice, and the feel of his legs as I rubbed against them."

Homer is, of course, a blind cat.

....

"*Ordo Amoris,*" I said, "I've been thinking about that." I'd been reading the philosopher Max Scheler. I read all sorts of things. Even if I don't always understand very much of what's involved. And I admit I was showing off... to a koala. *And in a dream, at that.*

"Sure, mate, sure," he replied.

"You know what that means?"

"I've got a pretty good idea, mate. I'm involved, my koala sweethearts and relatives are involved.... (*sigh*, or possibly a sigh), you're involved too, mate."

"But how do you know all this?"

"I suppose you think koalas just hang out on gum trees, eat gum leaves and sleep a lot?"

"Well, *yeah.*"

He paused. "I love the Australian bush, mate, especially the gum trees and the eucalyptus leaves. I love to eat the gum leaves, of course. I love the sunlight and the dark of night.... Some things, mate, I love more than others, of course, And some I *hate*: bush fires, needless to say. And people who are cruel to us, hurt or even kill us for 'fun'!" He was getting more and more excited as he went on. "I hated being on that ship! AND I HATE BEING IN HERNE BAY!"

I paused before saying anything.

"I can't help feeling I'm somehow projecting human emotions and ideas onto you..."

"Or am I trying to see you as a koala, mate?"

"But what does it relate to in the end? *Ordo Amoris*, I mean."

"Norman would insist on saying 'the Great Spirit Koala.' I just say 'the Great Spirit.'"

"Well, I guess that's ecumenical."

"None of your cheek, mate!"

"Do you really know what 'ecumenical' means?"

"I have a fair idea!"

"There are all sorts of things that are going to make you think of the Great Spirit," he said after a pause.

"But I never have...."

"Aw, but you will!"

He paused.

"The Great Spirit doesn't ever die, even if everything else does."

"Eternal, you mean?"

"Yeah, mate; that's it."

He paused.

"I once thought about writing something called 'On the Eternal in Koalas.'"

"You're having me on!"

"Aw, yeah, of course I am. You don't seriously think I can write, do you?"

"Well, you can *talk*!"

"Only to you, mate, only to you. And maybe Cyn."

"*Cyn*? What on earth are you talking about, Iredell?"

"You know, mate, Norm used to talk about the 'Communion of Koalas.' It was about tapping into the Great Spirit Koala and sharing in this. I guess I'd call it the 'Communion of the Great Spirit.'"

"Can humans be involved in this?"

"Aw, maybe, mate. But let's not get too carried away."

....

Another dream:

"Aw, koala mums are great, Dom. They're loving, they're really patient, and they'll protect their joeys no matter what!"

"Please stop calling me Dom! And as it happens, *my* mother was rather wonderful."

"So why don't you like females, mate?"

"I *do*! I like women!"

"Not from where I sit, Dom."

"And what do you know about it?"

"Well, are you with anyone now?"

"No, but..."

"When was the last time you were with someone? A year ago? Two years?"

"No, but..."

"Just as I thought, mate. Just as I thought."

I have to confess that I find women strange. But then I find men strange. I even find *myself* strange. Women are strange yet desirable: some, at least. Men are just strange. I'm strange and – as I know from experience – undesirable. At any rate, to anyone I'd be interested in. Except someone like Isabelle, but perhaps not even to her.

What do I mean by "strange"? Not that there's anything necessarily wrong with the individuals concerned. I suppose I just don't understand them. Or myself, for that matter; or other guys.

"But look," I said, "I'm obviously not going to feel about a girlfriend the way I felt about my mother."

Iredell frowned, at least as far as it's possible for a koala to do so.

"*Obviously*, mate! That's not the point I'm trying to make. Why don't you actually *like* females?"

I sighed. And woke up.

But not before I heard Iredell saying, "I'll send you a dream you'll *really* like, mate."

....

I hadn't even wanted to say to Iredell that gay men love their mothers, and they're... well, *gay*. But then it is a cliché, and moreover a misleading one in some instances at least: there are gays who loathe their mothers, others who are ambivalent towards them, and so on....

....

Ah yes, I did dream: of being in a crowded train carriage. And a voice – Iredell's – saying, "She's over there, mate." There was a woman, a really beautiful woman, sitting by herself: tall, svelte, red haired, with wonderful bone structure in both face and body. She looked at me expectantly. I went over and sat next to her. She smiled. I woke.

....

She was the most beautiful woman at the party – by a long ways. I couldn't believe she'd come over to talk to me.

I could hardly believe I was at the party: I hated them. I always felt awkward and out of place. But a friend had persuaded me to turn up. (*Awkward and out of place?* I'm a writer, I'm not supposed to use clichés like that. However, this is my story, and I'll do as I please. Besides, I can't think of anything better.)

I also couldn't believe she was the woman from my dream. But I'd swear she was.

Oh, God, I put so much stress on physical beauty at times!

"Hello, I'm Cynthia," she said. She offered me a cigarette, which I declined, then lit a cigarette and exhaled smoke through her nostrils. "I'm a performance artist. Oh, and I work as a legal secretary. And I'm interested in totem animals. Mine is a moon bear. What's your name?"

"My name's Dom," I said. After a pause I added: "My totem animal is a koala." I paused again, and then I said emphatically: "*I want to be a koala.*"

"Oh good!" she exclaimed. "*I want to be a moon bear!*"

And she bit me.

I won't say the obvious, but love was involved.

I should add it was more of a playful nibble than anything else, and my right ear was the object of her nibbling.

I decided not to say anything about how moon bears don't have red head-fur.

"How would you like to help me free a koala trapped in Herne Bay in a time warp?" I asked.

"Let's do it!"

She was obviously mad: as mad as I am. Oh God! What bliss!

....

Iredell wasn't wrong. She may have been – and is – a little crazy by certain standards, but she was also – and is – a gentle and genuinely sympathetic person. And she knew a thing or two, let us say. *Knows*, let us say further.

And yes, furthermore, *a good person*: as you'll see.

But I digress... or possibly anticipate....

I kept asking myself, *Why me?*

....

It was Cynthia who really did the research. She read old newspaper accounts, discovered clues in books... none of it terribly revealing on its own, but it all added up. We concluded that there really had been a koala colony in Herne Bay in the very early 1800s, and that the koalas had escaped.

....

The next time Iredell presented himself in one of my dreams, I said: "We think we know what you have to do. There's a river near Herne Bay, it's actually The River of Time...."

"I knew from my spirit dreams it was something like that. So I wouldn't just drown....?"

"No, no, we don't think so! We think David and Norman both emerged from it in another period of time! Cynthia's been doing a lot of reading, and she's almost positive about this."

"Aw, mate, I think that does make sense! So if I jump into that river, I'd come out of it in your time?"

"Well, possibly... but it might be any time at all."

"*What the bloody good would that do me?!*"

"Sorry. We'll work on it some more."

....

Cynthia did indeed do some more research.

And the next time Iredell popped up in one of my dreams, I said: "There are no magical formulae. You just have to put your trust in the Great Spirit Koala."

"*What?!*"

"OK, in the Great Spirit, if you prefer."

"*What?!*"

"Will you please stop saying that? We're doing the best we can here."

I paused.

"OK," I said, "we know it might not work. But it's a possibility. A *good* possibility, in more than one sense – that's what we think, anyway."

He seemed to shrug, and then made a sound like a sigh. (I'm trying to avoid anthropomorphism.)

"Yeah, mate," he said. "I'll try it."

"The river's not actually in Herne Bay, though: you'll have to travel some distance to get there...."

"Yeah, mate, I already have a fair idea where it is... and the spirit dreams will keep guiding me."

"But it's *some* distance, Iredell. I'm not sure you can do it...."

"Aw, mate, if other koalas have done it, so can I!"

....

"What will we actually do if Iredell shows up? We couldn't return him to Australia. And we couldn't keep him."

"Why not?" asked Cynthia.

"Well, neither of us has a eucalyptus tree. We'd have to give him to a zoo. And I don't think he'd like that."

"Listen, Dom. I've saved quite a lot of money, and it's been in my mind for some while to buy my own place. I'll find one with a eucalyptus tree already there."

"Is that likely?"

"It's certainly not impossible! I'll start looking today. And I don't mind if I end up having to commute – I've always done my best thinking about performances while travelling on trains."

"But it will take time! And Iredell doesn't have time – he's hiding out!"

"I can cut some corners, I'm fairly sure of that. As a legal secretary I've acquired some useful contacts. Don't worry so much!"

"So you'll keep Iredell, and I'll – "

"You can come and stay at weekends, at least to begin with." She paused.

"And after a while, we can also adopt a moon bear!"

"Isn't that impossible?"

"Is it any more impossible than us adopting a koala?"

"Cynthia," I said, "I'm not the best looking guy around, and I haven't done very much...."

"Be quiet," she said. "You're imperfectly lovely."

"But I've always wanted to know... why did you approach me at that party?"

"You looked shy, and I've found that shy people are often gentle, and I like that."

"There must have been something more..."

"Well, if you really want to know, it was because you look like George Stubbs. You could be his brother!"

"*Who?*"

"You know, the painter of horses. I've always been fascinated by him."

Well, I thought, better than being told I'm fat, pimply and degenerate-looking. Or not just degenerate-looking, but downright *degenerate*.

"You didn't also have a dream about me, by any chance?"

"Of course not, Dom. What a silly question!"

"Just checking," I said.

I'd moved from Notting Hill to Finsbury Park, in North London, and lost track of Ray. I'd tried to contact him, but to no avail. By this time he'd long left the halfway house and the forwarding address he'd given them was either phoney or out-of-date. I wished I hadn't left it for such a time before trying.

And then Ray wrote to me, his letter forwarded from two previous addresses. He'd come into a legacy and had moved to Greece.

"I was in prison again," Ray wrote. "But shortly after my release, my Aunt Joanna died and her legacy came through. And I've always wondered about Greece, somehow. Especially after you went there that time, when I saw you off at the airport. So here I am."

....

Why would I want to go to Greece? Yes, to see Ray. Yes, because it's one of the places I've felt most at home: something I can't even begin to disentangle from friendships, memories, and so forth. And of course, amongst those friendships and memories: Bob Lax.

I suppose one of the most important things about Bob – for me – was his tendency towards *non-entanglement*. What do I mean by this? I mean that he never tried to entangle me in his own ways and ideas. He was as he was as a poet and person, and he clearly respected that I should be as I am, or as I would become.

Perhaps I should also have said: as Bob was becoming. For he never stopped searching: though he wasn't "seeking", at least in Ray's sense.

Let's quote from something of his:

Searching for you, but if there's no one, what am I searching for? Still you. Some sort of you. Not for myself? Am I you? Need I search for me? Is my self you? I know: Self. Is that you? Is it me?

(...)

I go on searching. I was born for that.

(...)

My person. My beloved, if you like: my sought-after-being, my remembered-one, would be there. The one I'd looked for, the one I'd sought without any clear idea of who he or she might be, of what he or she might look like, would appear.

That's from something entitled '21 pages.' It might be glossed thus:

        hide-

        &-

        go-

        seek

        I

        you

spirit

the

spirit

In hermeneutics, it might be seen as the interplay of hiddenness and revealing: what can never be fully revealed, must be partially hidden (as part of a dialogue, so to speak). But what is it? You. Me. Or: perhaps what Iredell calls the Great Spirit. Should that be *and* as well as *or*? Yes. We could say: both within the person, *and* without (*and* beyond); within experience, *and* transcendent to it. But not what Hope meant by "spirits" – or at least, the way she made use of the idea of "spirits".

But it's always down to particulars. Not abstractions. (Was I using abstractions?)

I sensed that for Bob Lax small things, small details, mattered. Why else did Bob often write one syllable to a line, caring about each and every syllable? Why else did he care for the stray cats on Patmos, where he lived for many years, when no one else was bothering?

My sense of Bob was that he was someone who was always learning. And that's how I feel, and maybe that's what he did teach me. (And what he was able to teach.) But it was a very *individual* lesson, and more, also, about *sharing in something* than in passing on verities, or anything like that.

It also had something to do with *attention*... a certain sort of attention.

"Attentiveness is the rarest and purest form of generosity," wrote Simone

Weil; and it is the gentle yet strong focus, lucidity and faithfulness of the act of attention (to words, to the things and the people around him, to whatever he names in poems) that constitutes one of the most salient features of Lax's poetry and also his life.

This involved probing, questioning, and yes, states of mind, insights... and remaining fundamentally open-ended in your searching.

He definitely didn't set himself up as some sort of "spiritual master". Whatever else, that would have demanded a lineage, such as any Zen Buddhist or Greek Orthodox priest would tell you. Nor was he a "saint", at least in the sense of a *spiritual athlete* or *hero*. Perhaps, as in the Jewish tradition which he was born into and possibly never really fully abandoned, he *cleaved to God*: *devukut*.

What he shared with others was a fellowship in friendship, in poetry and in the Spirit.

And perhaps that joins up with a Christian notion, that of the Co-inherence or Communion of Saints. ("Saints" as fellow believers, not "spiritual athletes," and possibly just all those somehow embraced in the Spirit, regardless of dogma and unnecessary divisiveness.) Dear Bob Lax, may you truly cleave to God, and I, also, and let us meet now and later more fully in the Co-inherence.

Oh dear! I sound like I'm echoing something Iredell said, or some adaptation of it!

Perhaps I've been learning from him, after all....

....

Is "Petros" the poet Robert Lax, known to his friends as Bob? Yes. Is "Benny Silverstein" me? More or less: yes, more or less.

I recall quite distinctly, quite vividly even, what happened when I left Patmos in that October of 1973.

We were on Patmos, as I've said, and the sea was unusually rough, so that the ships were not stopping there, though they were stopping at the nearby island of Leros. I had to get back to Athens, to catch a bus back to London. Bob hired a launch to take me to Leros. Now, we'd been under surveillance all the time we'd been on Patmos: the Patmian chief of police and his second-in-command had come over in the ship from Kalymnos with us, they'd stayed at the same hotel (either the Rex or the Crystal – there were only two of them at the time), and they spent their time in the hotel lounge, dressed in white with white hats but with dark glasses, and looked at us whenever we went out. So far, so... well, it turned out that Bob was considered an American spy (he went around talking to the islanders and writing strange things in his notebooks – experimental poems which looked like code to the cops, except they couldn't break it). His house had been searched, and informants had been delegated to attach themselves to him. I knew nothing of this. I hate to admit that I knew next to nothing about the horrific reign of the Greek Colonels.

Ah, but when I was about to leave, the second-in-command jumped on board the launch with the skipper and me, and off we went. It was a rough crossing, no doubt about that: I'm a fairly good sailor, but on this crossing I was violently sick and then passed out. When I woke, they were talking together, in Greek; and we were approaching Leros... not the harbour, no, the other side of the island. We docked. There was a car waiting there, and I was, let's say, *steered* into it: the Greek police, of course. Off we went. I had the insouciance of youth on my side: I was unaware of any danger. I was stupid, of course. But lucky.

So, we drove. There was some discussion in Greek, presumably about what to do with me. Finally, someone looked back to the rear seat where I was sitting, and asked: "Do you want to go to a hotel?"

"No," I said, "I'll be leaving the island this evening."

More discussion amongst themselves, but not with me.

"Do you want to go to a restaurant?"

I thought about this. I was hungry, so I said "Yes."

Indeed, they dropped me off at a restaurant, and also dropped off one of their men to keep an eye on me.

It was one of those places where you're invited into the kitchen to see what's on offer. I chose the moussaka. It was the best I've *ever* had, then or now.

And I caught the next ship to Piraeus.

....

Ray had settled into Athens and seemed to know it well... as a thief would, you might possibly say. I stayed in his modest flat, sleeping on a sofa, and we'd take daytime and night time walks together, stopping at cafés and tavernas, strolling off again, eventually returning to the flat to rest or to sleep.

Ray stopped outside a door during one of our walks and pointed to it. "There's a Greek philosopher lives here", he said. "He's something of a follower of Hans-Georg Gadamer, or so I hear."

"You know about Gadamer? And a Greek thinker who's influenced by him?" I asked.

Ray shrugged.

"Hermeneutics," he said. "Interpretation and understanding: isn't that what it's mainly about?" He paused. "And perhaps it's to do with messages." He paused again. "I don't suppose I really understand much of what someone like Gadamer's on about...."

"Hermes again!" And, for goodness sake, hermeneutics!

"Better than being a thief, Dominic. And I've always liked to read. I'd read your stories if you'd let me, but you never have! What about now, though?"

"There's a problem there, Ray. I can't seem to finish any of them!"

"Ah!"

"But I have a new girlfriend, and I think you'd like her."

"That's good to hear!"

"And we're adopting a koala."

His face fell. Oh dear, I thought, I must work on this! But how?

"She identifies with moon bears."

If at all possible, his face fell further.

"She's really nice," I said.

I decided to change the subject.

"Have you read Max Scheler?" I asked.

"Of course," he said.

Hmm.

"That's what I did when I was last in prison: read, I mean, but more seriously than I ever had before. My aunt helped, sending me books I wanted. I found I knew far less than I thought I did, but I was eager to learn. I read and read, and I did learn."

"You haven't started writing as well, have you?"

"Oh yes! I've just finished my first novel."

Hmm.

"I've looked at all the literature, and I established a narrative arc for my novel."

"*What?!*"

"Oh come on, you know what a narrative arc is, Dominic. It's basic, surely. I bet you use them in your fiction."

"*My* stories never get as far as needing anything like an arc, arch, circle or triangle, Ray."

"Hmm," he said.

....

"This is our champagne," said Bob, holding up a large bottle of mineral water. He was as I remembered, tall, rather gangly, with a long, thin face and sparse hair, and a friendly smile.

Just the same.... Oh dear, I thought: water!

But at least it was sparkling mineral water.

"By the way, I have a new girlfriend," I said.

"That's good," said Bob, and smiled.

"And we're adopting a koala."

"*Really*?" he said, and laughed.

I decided not to say anything about moon bears.

As far as I know, Bob hadn't been involved in sexual or romantic relationships since his early adulthood, when he went out with a young woman named Nancy Flagg: she eventually married his friend Robert Gibney.

It had been a choice, as far as I understood him. And why not? Why not, indeed?

....

I did meet a woman who might or might not have also been a former girlfriend of Bob's, but had at the very least been a close friend. When Bob was a clown – a clown for loan, not for keeps, you might say – with the Cristiani Family Circus, she picked out his name for him: Cesco, from Francesco (Saint Francis). Apt. She was living in London, in a mansion flat, having married into money, and a couple of friends of Bob's persuaded me to phone her and invite myself over, because they knew she had some early poems of his and nobody had been able to get hold of them. I suppose they thought I was young and charming. I was young, at any rate. And naïve: innocent, perhaps. She plied me with wine, which she was drinking freely, and we talked, and talked, and at the end of the evening, without my asking, she handed me copies of the poems in question. She must have had them made in advance. I kid you not. Why? *Why indeed?* Perhaps she just liked the sound of my voice on the phone. I'll never know. I was too drunk to ask and never thought to later on.

I slept in her husband's bed that night (he was away on business) and she slept in her own. She'd insisted on giving me a bottle of wine to take to bed with me.

In the morning I heard her say, as I was waking, "Oh, darling, you're back! There's a man in your bed."

I met him, and he didn't like me. I had long hair. He thought that showed lack of "backbone".

So it goes.

....

I'd seen Bob, I'd seen Ray. I needed to get back to London. Cynthia awaited me. And, in Herne Bay, or rather, near it: Iredell.

....

Perhaps Cynthia is also "the right artist," like Box Lax, as well as a good person.... or at least, *one sort of right artist.*

I was finally able to attend one of her performances, which were (and are) infrequent.

It was a small gallery, which had been darkened so that the only illumination came from a number of small coloured beams of light projected through bear-shaped stencil patterns cut into pieces of cardboard. We sat on the floor or on chairs at the entrance to the space, which had been festooned with paper cut-outs in the form of moon bears. (Are you getting the idea yet?) Veils and mirrors had been arranged in strategic places, and mirrors also covered the floor. Slow, quiet trance music played on a tape machine. Cynthia appeared, dressed in a costume that indeed suggested a moon bear while doing nothing to disguise her slender and elegant figure, and began a very slow, purposively awkward and bear-like dance around the space, taking full advantage of the lights, mirrors and veils. Every now and again she chanted: "Captive moon bear, be free! Free moon bear, live well! Dead moon bear, be at peace!"

It lasted about half an hour. It should have been ridiculous and laughable. But it wasn't. I found myself thoroughly entranced, and even moved.

....

A koala was swimming across the river; I recognised him: it was Iredell, of course. Cynthia and I were there too, in a skiff. He stopped swimming and began to sink, but not before he was within reach. I scooped him up from the water and put him down in the boat.

"Aw, thanks, mate," he said. "Thanks, Cyn."

He caught his breath, looking around him and clearly thinking about things – he had that look.

And this time it wasn't a dream.

True Points

"...the only true point is a turning point." (F E Sparshott)

The child pressed her face to the window of the bus; breathed upon it; and wrote with her finger.

Walking from the bus-stop to my house, I followed in the wake of litter, scraps of paper blown by the wind.

"You remember I called? Philippa?" she said.

"Of course," I said; and invited her to come inside.

The young woman's eyes were frank when they met mine, but they did so rarely, for the most part looking to the side. Her smile (lips closed) creased the left cheek, infusing her features with geniality.

"I must admit," I said, "how surprised I was that Tony would think of giving anyone my address; it's been years since we were in touch."

"Oh, he told me I *had* to look you up!" she said, quite unabashed by my remark.

"And I was glad he did," she continued; "it's good to have someone to visit when you're in a strange country."

I had no idea who she might be. But she talked on, telling of her travels and the people she'd met during her time abroad, as if to a friend; and it disarmed me, and I was touched. Nothing she said was out of the ordinary, yet I felt no wish to cut her visit short.

After Philippa left, I spent an hour or so trying to put some of my papers in order. I couldn't settle to it.

No work was done that night.

* * *

"The chivalrous people of old," Mike said later. "Valorous, too – I wouldn't be surprised."

"What did they say to make you think so?" I asked.

"Ah! so you needed to hear them *say* something!"

The elderly couple had attended to us through the merest nod, smile or gesture, with only the occasional word (kindly and sufficient); it was left to their children and in-laws to minister to our needs. They had, it seemed, passed on the obligation of speech to the younger men and women; who in turn obeyed it with discretion. The sublime ease of these people, and their hospitality towards strangers, impressed us both. Obviously, they were poor, as the furnishings and neglect of their cottage revealed. What did they do, in the way of work? I asked one of the younger men this question, and he replied simply: "We're fishermen."

A young woman, conspicuous because of the baby at her breast, sat at one end of the table, her face suffused with the firelight. I noticed the quiet, sympathetic interest she took in us, her family's guests. She listened closely when Michael told an anecdote about once sharing a hospital ward with a professor of architectural history – a brilliant man, Mike said. One day the professor stopped speaking in the middle of an account of his student days in Rome, and began flapping his arms energetically, as if to drive something away.

"What's the matter?" Michael had asked his companion.

"Those birds!" he'd said; "you've let those birds in!"

There was nothing in the room; but Michael had to wave his arms at the hallucinatory birds, until finally the professor closed the window to seal their departure.

I wondered at Mike for telling these stories; surely he realized how much he was giving away about himself. No one, it was true, showed any alteration towards us; yet I felt the need of the cold night air again.

We took a path that led up a hill, shoes sucking in the thick mud; the darkness virtually complete. We were talking, for the sake of continuity in unfamiliar surroundings; and I recalled the tower-block where I'd visited Mike during the first years of our friendship. "– Summer," I said; "sun upon the windows. I'd look up from the street to your window; the glass rectangles pulsating against their frames. The neighbouring black roofs were blinding."

Our voices were the only sound for a half-an-hour or more, until a sudden hubbub of dogs' barking broke out at no great distance. The noise abated after a few minutes; but we decided to go down the hill again and find where we'd left the car.

* * *

The burly tramp in the dirty grey overcoat might have been mistaken for her Uncle Robert, Philippa said, except that Robert was dead; the resemblance was unnerving. He'd slipped to his knees on the pavement; I took his arm and helped him to his feet.

Uncle Robert, she told me, had been a professional boxer in his youth. Seldom sober, even so his skill had let him win many of his matches.

By the time of Philippa's adolescence, Robert was a confirmed alcoholic, utterly dependent upon his relatives and his few friends in every way. He'd smile obligingly for his niece's camera from the fat and grizzled countenance of his waste.

She recalled talking with him once about her Aunt Lucy, who had developed a blood clot in her throat from which she could die any day. She mentioned her difficulty in talking with Lucy, since there was painfully little in the way of shared concerns. "You could talk to her about boxing," Robert had said.

"You could tell her," he'd continued, "about Jimmy Carruthers...." And he talked about a film of Carruthers fighting in Bangkok, with magisterial skill and grace, in defence of the championship; barefoot in the open-air ring flooded from the monsoon rain and littered with debris.

We were having lunch in a café; and I talked about my friendship with Tony; telling her how, at a time of great loneliness, he'd come into my life (through a mutual acquaintance) to be the one person with whom I then felt any large accord.

"Does he still live in that house near the railway viaduct, with the large back garden? I was visiting him one day – this was when he was still married to Jan – and there was a point during the afternoon when I left the house to go out into the garden by myself and sit there, on the ground. The garden, the quiet of the afternoon, Tony and Jan's friendship – these things came together to make me feel strangely peaceful – for it was a troubled period in my life. I was sitting so that I faced a sapling, and I sat there a long time looking at it; and I suddenly felt borne back, throughout my whole body and self, to... well, what should I say? a first state both tender and guiltless."

"Charles!" Philippa said, laughing; "you're really strange!"

In the evening I returned home, to write.

My front room faced out towards a waste square where tenements had recently stood; hollows, planes and lights of the large building behind were framed by dark forms of foliage – night's changes absorbed the squalor.

It was at this time that I was able to write.

I'd become caught up in the idea of a co-incidence of opposites: of image and imagelessness, visibility and invisibility, finitude and infinitude; and it had brought me to the threshold of a darkened chamber – I had entered, and sat down. I wanted to see, and to pursue in reflection, the way in which divine Being *is revealed in every being and yet always hidden in them.* Notes were compiled; and left in folders; more notes were written; and I felt lost in the process and act.

***

Sitting at the car's wheel, Mike handed me a road-map; although it was too dark to read it.

"Where now?" he said, and smiled broadly.

We drove inland; and stopped for the night at a run-down hotel.

"The Hesperian Hotel!" said Michael. The name was sufficiently quaint, I surmised, to please my friend.

We took turns showering in a narrow cubicle. When I had finished I went to our room, where I found Mike reading in bed. I slipped in beneath the covers of my own bed and waited for Mike to begin talking: for he always wanted to converse for a while before sleep.

"...and they would tear live flesh with their teeth," said Mike.

"Or", I said, "the living substance of other people. *Sparagmos*. Such a polite word."

"And you, you care too much for words!"

"Michael," I said, "would you turn out the light now?"

Once in darkness, we were both silent for several minutes. Then I began speaking again.

"How easy to mask evil," I said, "with a multitude of disguises. But good, too..."

"Good?"

"...is hidden from us; camouflaged. You know it when it has pierced you with wound after wound."

***

The first leaves were lit from beneath, leaves of the second tree full on by lamplight; the facade of the hotel lit, in part, by its own lights. And from behind – a voice rising in song, its distance increasing with my steps – plaintive song.

I found the door of Philippa's house, a little further, in a row of terraces. The street was quiet at that hour, but the stones were thick with dirt from demolition work being carried out across the road.

I was dismayed by how maculate and disordered a room I found myself entering. Papers, books, bedding and clothes were piled around without any attempt at arrangement. Table and sink were littered with unwashed plates and pans, cups and glasses.

A painful sense of dereliction caught at me.

But she led me by the hand into the room, and to a chair, apologising hastily for the mess, as she called it; then she moved away, to find herself a place to sit.

A photograph had been tacked to the wall, near the window. It was, I saw, a snapshot of Philippa, standing at the railings of a ship. She was smiling and waving.

When I re-entered the room, I saw that Philippa was leaning out the window, surveying the street below; with her head behind the thin green curtain. She lit a cigarette, and the match flame pricked a spot of the dull green alive.

***

I dreamt that Michael and I had gone to a party at Philippa's; we sat by ourselves, watching couples dancing, until Philippa came and drew Mike into the dance. A little later she came back to where I was sitting, and said: "Guess what I've come to ask you for?" "I don't know," I said. "A dance!" Philippa said; but I begged off, and went into another room.

"Put it on," someone said, handing me a waxen mask. As soon as it covered my face, he also gave me a long gown to wear. I saw now that the others in the room were similarly masked and attired.

We all went out in the street, and to an Underground station; the man who had given us masks and gowns then had us sit astride the poles by the escalator-stairs. An icy wind blew, from time to time, down the escalator. The man took out a small cine-camera from the bag he'd been carrying; he filmed us as we sat clinging to the poles; while the people descending past us on the stairs looked with amusement, or incomprehension, or even anger.

When we returned to the party, Philippa refused to speak to me – ignoring my greeting, and walking away. I followed her through the house; she shut a door, I opened it; she shut another door, I followed, and opened that too; until I pushed open the door to a room where Philippa, on her knees, naked, was being whipped by someone disguised with a mask.

Philippa turned her face to look directly at me as I entered, and she cried out.

Mike and I breakfasted at the hotel, where a large ground floor room had been set aside; part of it functioned as a kitchen, while tables and chairs (all, as it happened, empty save for our own table) occupied the rest of the space. The hour, Mike suggested, might explain the absence of other guests; for we had woken late.

We ate toast and marmalade, and drank tea. The quiet, and the warm sunshine, suffused us. It was too perfect; for it suddenly seemed to me the inversion of Philippa's cry.

"Two men, both in their early thirties," said Michael, "engaged upon some last desperate romantic quest, the details of which mostly remain obscure, needless to say...."

"The self-dramatising, though, would be more obvious?" I said. But Mike stood up, his chair falling back and hitting the pavement. He went into the café to order more coffee; when he returned, he picked the chair up and seated himself again.

"Son of a bitch," he said.

"I'm sorry," I said. Then: "Do you want to go back to the hotel for lunch, or shall we eat here?"

"I want to *talk* to you," he said.

***

Philippa took several peaches from a paper bag and placed them in a bowl on the table.

I was standing at the window, and happened to look down into the street; two big workmen had stopped their truck and were manoeuvring an injured cat from the road onto a large cardboard sheet. Traffic was building up behind them, yet they proceeded with a slow, caring patience.

"I was *always* falling in love at that time," Philippa said; "so often, that nothing else seemed to be happening. I was meeting all kinds of different men, at parties and at clubs; and often I'd be in love with several of them."

There was a vivacity to the young woman that I found charming; but there has always been a puritanical strain in my nature, and I was ill at ease when she began to talk about her love affairs.

"I believe in getting everything into my life," she said, as if to underline what she'd just told me. "Then," she continued after a pause, "if I look back there's a lot that doesn't seem important anymore."

"For all of us," I said. "There's a saying: 'So much chaff for the wind'".

Philippa had cut a peach into slices, which we were eating when her doorbell rang.

She left the room and entered again, bringing a tall, lean young man with her. He immediately walked over to me and extended his hand. "I'm Patrick," he said.

**

"Think of this," I said: "a stream alive with stones, driven mad by the sun. A young woman stands looking into the water, and the face of her long-dead brother appears beneath its surface. Like a stone that's awakened, but to unmitigated suffering.

"She hasn't thought of him," I continued, "for many years. A fulgurating sorrow for him strikes through her."

"*What* kind of a sorrow?" Mike asked.

"Never mind," I said. He was right: I love words too much. "She cries out:

'Whatever the risk, I will come and aid you!' And she keeps her thoughts on the child and his suffering until, in a dream, she sees him safe on ground, playing happily amongst other children."

A man at the next table turned to us and said:

"Perpetua. You haven't got her story right, did you know? She was in prison, awaiting martyrdom, and she had a vision of her brother who'd died many years before, as a child. (He had cancer of the face – isn't that terrible?) Anyway: instead of being immersed in water, as you thought, he was unable to drink from a pool, or a large vessel, it's also said: the brim was beyond his reach. But after Perpetua's prayers she saw him drinking the water; she also saw that his face had healed; and that he then began to play, because his suffering was over."

"Donald," he said. "You must come over to my place for a drink."

His gestures were implacably effeminate; his pale skin was flaking from obsessive washing (as he confessed readily enough); his eyes coquettish; his hair long and blond. He was highly erudite. While we looked through his snapshots (in which, characteristically, he posed with young men wearing leather motorcycle clothing, their motorbikes alongside or behind them), Donald conversed about a string of subjects, eccentrically linked; so that he moved from Arnald of Villanova's *The Time of the Coming of the Antichrist* to Apocalyptic themes in German Expressionism; and then to the vertiginous mysticism of the heretics of the Free Spirit.

When Mike went out to buy some cigarettes, Donald said to me: "He's so good-looking, isn't he? Is he your lover?"

"No," I said.

"Well," he said, "maybe you don't like such masculine men? Mind you, he *is* terribly nervy...."

I didn't have to answer, for he immediately got up and went to the bathroom.

When he came back, he said: "Do you think I'm weird? I mean, that I can't stand to feel unclean and have to wash so often? Does it make me seem crazy?"

I said: "It would only matter if you felt it harmed you in some essential way. It shouldn't make any difference at all to anyone else."

Michael came in the door then. Donald turned to him and said, pointing in my direction: "This man has been sent by Our Saviour to help me!"

Coming back to the hotel late in the evening, we stopped to peer through the window into the darkened interior of the dining-room, where a single lamp had been left burning, lighting up the area that served as the kitchen. Empty as the room was, there was a flame of hospitality that burned there, its light spreading over the kitchen's casual, yet cared-for, appearance.

I thought of the small kitchen-space within Donald's front room; with the glass sphere attached by thread to the ceiling, just above the rack of china plates. Donald had pinned up some other photographs of himself and his companions, with a postcard of Grünewald's Isenheim Altarpiece (showing the panel of the risen Christ) directly above them. And his voice, in memory, telling us more of Perpetua's story: how she dreamed of changing into a man, to fight with the Devil in the guise of an Egyptian warrior; and how she flung him down; and was rewarded with a branch of golden apples.

**

Philippa suddenly said: "When I was at college there were two tutors who started off having no respect for me at all; but by the time I finished the course, I had them eating out of the palm of my hand."

"What sort of course was it?" I asked.

"Catering," she said.

She talked in a way that was unfamiliar, prompted (it seemed) by her friend's presence, although he, for his part, scarcely spoke; and I felt a sadness penetrating me, as if soaking little by little throughout my body.

In the days when she and Patrick had first known each other, she had been working as a "hostess" in a nightclub. "You get these sleazy guys who think they can get what they want out of you," she said, "and it's up to you to get what you want out of *them*. It's only the natural and right thing; they deserve to be taken for their money.

"I got other things from them besides money, too," she continued. "They think if they give you drugs, or even if they just buy presents for you, you'll end up in their power. They don't have any respect for you, and that's why I didn't have any respect for them."

My eye wandered again to the window and the street below; but the two workmen had gone.

I looked at Patrick; I could see nothing in his face (nothing below or within the frame of jet-black hair), for I thought of him as a reflection of the many boyfriends she'd talked about. Leather jacket, T-shirt and jeans: the standard declaration of his dress supported this loss of differentiation.

"No more than shadows," Patrick said; or at least I thought him to say it.

"What?" I asked; for I wanted to be certain that the young man had said these words — which made me want to catch up and comfort the very shadows.

"What *what*?" Patrick replied, looking at me askance.

I couldn't see him; I heard him, and didn't hear him.

***

I showered and returned to the room. Michael was already in bed; he turned his head to look at me as I came in the door.

I signed to Mike that I wanted to write something in my notebook (the phrases had been running through my head all the while I was washing myself), and he took up his book again.

"You remember what it was like?" he said. "I'd come out of the hospital, but

I was scarcely able to talk to anyone, or make a decision for myself, or in fact do much at all."

"I remember."

"What was it like? It was like I was cycling through an orchard with every tree dense with birds, and the birds were shitting on me as I cycled beneath them.

"And do you remember the big storm late that autumn?" he continued.

"Yes, I remember it."

"I expected that the faces of all the people I've ever loved who have died would come to me in the night. I expected to wake up covered in blood; I thought it was a judgement! In the morning there were heaps of sodden leaves collected by the wind, uprooted trees, smashed windows, flooded gutters...."

When I eventually got to sleep, I dreamt that Philippa and I were travelling together by boat, in a sea fiery with the sun's reflection. Classical sculptures – figures of the gods – rose from the water on either side of the vessel, and I said: "Let's hope we don't hit any of the statues." Philippa smiled, and said: "Think of it: a woman stands there, looking into the water...."

***

Philippa was the only person who'd had an opportunity to take the things (a brooch and a necklace of my mother's, which I had kept in my desk-drawer since her death). I disliked the idea of Philippa having stolen them, but no other conclusion seemed possible.

I went to see her, and we talked for some time before I said:

"Philippa, my mother's jewellery's been taken from my flat."

"No one cares," she said, "if I've got enough to eat, or if my clothes are in rags. You don't care, Charles!"

"You should have said something. Philippa, you must know I feel a great deal of sympathy for you...."

"I don't want your fucking sympathy," she said.

I lost my temper then. "You're a treacherous little bitch," I said.

"So are you!" she shouted. And, raising her voice even more: "Get out of here!"

She opened the door, but stood in the doorway so that it was impossible to get past her.

"If our bodies grew so bright we could see through to each other's secrets.... That's a dream, but from heaven," I said.

"From fucking hell!" she said. "Do you think I *want* to know your dirty little secrets, or that I'd want you to fucking-well know mine?"

"If we *could* see each other in that way," I said, "we'd weep with each other;

that's all."

Philippa stepped to one side. "Get out of here", she said.

I walked until I came to a small park; I went in, and sat down on a bench. Shafts of light and moisture in the air composed an envelope for silence; the kind of silence that follows in the wake of pandemonium, and encloses anguish.

To the memory of Petros Bourgos.

The King's Three Bodies

Chapter 1:

Archie

Archie was as gentle and benign as anyone could wish, even though for a wombat he was surprisingly large. His size didn't incline him to aggression, not in the least; if anything it added passivity to his good nature.

Passive, did I say? Yes, on the whole. However, there was more to Archie than one might think: as we shall see. Also, the wombats in his particular wisdom or group may indeed be gentle on the whole, and I do say *on the whole*, but if provoked they can react in measure. "Retaliate, in other words?" I hear someone say. Yes.

And Mr Archie, as he preferred to be called, lived of course in Australia, way out in the outback. As Australians would say, it was way out woop woop; so much so that mentioning the area's name would be pointless. I'll only just say that it was in a remote part of Victoria: way out there.

Scrub, mainly. And dirt. Scree. More dirt, further out. But there were also a few areas that were more arable, though mostly amounting to shrubland: at the sheep station, for instance, or at Pastor Bob's Mission. A cluster of homesteads, mostly belonging to the people who worked at the sheep station but didn't live there. A pub. A general store.

Unlike most wombats, Mr Archie forbore burrowing; he didn't even walk around that much: he preferred to sit, whenever possible, preferably on someone's lap.

That someone was Pastor Bob.

At the Lutheran Mission for Wombats, Mr Archie had been taught by Pastor Bob to read and write, and to believe in Jesus Christ. He also knew a little geometry and even a little bit of trigonometry. And he could paint. And he could sing. He could sing beautifully, in fact, in a rich tenor voice. He was a well-educated wombat, was Mr Archie.

How did he come to be there? The word had gotten around amongst the wombats: that there was an exceptionally kind man who seemed to really like their kind, who encouraged them to stay at his place, and to eat there, and didn't even disapprove of a little burrowing. And he'd set up a sort of school for them – imagine such a thing! So Mr Archie joined the other wombats at Pastor Bob's.

"Can we go on digging burrows, and still be Christians?" he'd asked Pastor Bob.

"*Of course,*" replied Pastor Bob. But Mr Archie and the other wombats found that after a while they didn't want to.

"Mr Archie," said Pastor Bob one day, "we must have a little talk."

Mr Archie nodded as if in agreement, though truth to tell he didn't know what Pastor Bob wanted to discuss; not at all.

"But before we do, shall we read *Sixpence to Spend*? Shall I read it to you, as a tiny treat?"

Mr Archie nodded enthusiastically. *Sixpence to Spend* was one of his favourite books. Someone might protest that *Sixpence to Spend* is a children's story. Would such people consider that Mr Archie should have been reading Descartes, perhaps, or Pascal? He was only a wombat, after all, however talented. Pastor Bob and Mr Archie would both have been hard put to say exactly why they loved

Sixpence to Spend, the story of a little koala, so much. They much preferred it to dreadful old Norman Lindsay's *The Magic Pudding*. Dreadful? He was clearly anti-Semitic. And then as an artist, there were those countless tediously similar female nudes; and that horrible Crucifixion with crowds of degenerate cavorting Romans giving the thumbs down sign.

Young koalas are indeed favourites of humans… well, *many* humans… and wombats alike. Having said that, I should add that Mr Archie's experience of koalas was somewhat limited. But he knew what he liked. And he was right to like koalas.

"You know I'd never leave you and the others, don't you?" said the Pastor, after he'd finished reading the story.

Mr Archie nodded.

"I'm going to have to leave you."

Mr Archie shook his head in dismay. He began to feel dizzy.

"I have a confession to make, my dear friend."

He breathed a deep sigh.

"They said to me, 'You were sent there to convert the Aboriginal Australians' – that's the black people here – 'not to set up a mission for *wombats*! How can marsupials understand anything about faith? Besides, you led us to believe you'd been offered a position in an existing church with a congregation – just one that needed some funding. Now we find you built a ramshackle place yourself from scrap, and we hear that the congregation consists *entirely* of wombats! This is sheer insanity… you've clearly taken leave of your senses.' Yes, they said all that, and more. The upshot is that I've been recalled to England to face these… *charges* – in person."

Pastor Bob paused, and let out a long sigh.

"I don't know how long I'll be away, or even if they'll let me come back at all."

He paused again.

"I'm afraid it's true that I lied to them for a long time about what I was really doing. I did use much of my own money, for sure, but I used theirs as well. I'm not sorry, mind you. I'm certain that what I was doing was thoroughly worthwhile!"

Mr Archie nodded.

"I'm leaving you in charge, Mr Archie, in charge of the wisdom and also in charge of the Mission, at least while I'm away. You'll be… in a sense… the *king*. You know, like in the stories I've told you about the Knights of the Round Table."

Why would I be a king? Mr Archie asked himself.

Almost as if he'd read his thoughts, Pastor Bob said: "You have a better singing voice than any of the others, you're more intelligent, you've a thoroughly agreeable personality…. And besides… there's your dexterity…."

Mr Archie looked up at Pastor Bob, who nodded to him.

Mr Archie waddled over to the table and chairs. He hoisted himself onto a chair and managed a sitting position, then reached out and closed his paw around the paperknife and lifted it. He then relaxed his paw to drop the implement.

"Now," said Pastor Bob, "what other wombat can do *that*?"

Chapter 2:

Pastor Bob's Story

Mr Archie hadn't yet been born when Pastor Bob was ordained.

But why would anyone want to know about Pastor Bob's earlier life?

Because of this story. It's necessary to know more about Pastor Bob in order to understand how things started… and to some extent how they developed.

Let's just say his life had been somewhat… rackety? Irregular? Odd?

He'd been a bookseller, and after that a librarian. Oh, and other things besides. But he had no ambition at all and therefore never achieved any standing in any profession.

One day he decided he wanted to go to a church. Which church? Why?

Let's back track.

He'd read an article. In a popular magazine. He was almost ashamed he read the rag. Well, they had reasonable (he thought)… well, *you* know, men want to meet women, women want to meet men, and so on… *columns*.

It turned out the women, who were all rather… ordinary? shall we say?… thought they'd meet incredibly handsome and successful men, who for some reason would immediately drool over them.

Pastor Bob was not incredibly handsome nor successful.

Did he go to church because of this? No.

But he was feeling disillusioned.

Let's backtrack further.

Pastor Bob had been married.

It hadn't been a happy marriage. And there'd been no children.

A fairly amicable divorce.

He decided to experiment. With blind dates.

And then with religion.

Experiment, that's to say, in going to various churches and seeing how he felt about them.

The very first one was a Lutheran Church not all that far from where he lived in London.

Traditional Lutheran choral vespers. A little like Gregorian chant. Another week, jazz vespers. A very good tenor sax player sometimes performed there, to Bob's amazement and pleasure. And on other weeks, Bach vespers… a service with music by Bach of course, but also Buxtehude, Biber and others.

Bob began going there on a regular basis, almost every Sunday, in fact. No reason to go anywhere else.

He even took part in the readings.

And then his mother died. (His father had died much earlier.)

"We should have a memorial service for her," said Pastor Jasna.

"Oh yes," said Bob. "Please."

"You were close to her?"

Bob nodded.

"Ever since you've been coming here, I've sensed a considerable unhappiness about you," she said.

"True, true: I've never really felt satisfied about anything... anything at all."

"And I must say I've noticed that you've been a little... *inebriated* some of the times you've been here."

"True," said Bob. "I'm sorry, Pastor Jasna."

"Well, we *are* Lutherans, not Baptists! But do try to get your drinking under control, Bob, please."

"I *can* get the drinking under control, really I can."

"Bob," said Pastor Jasna, "I'm thinking about all this dissatisfaction in your life: have you ever thought you might possibly have a *calling*?"

Chapter 3:

Pastor Bob and the Outback Pub… Sometime
after His Arrival and Sometime before His Departure

"Struth, mate, I'm tellin' ya Young Griffo was the first bloody Aussie to be world champ!"

"Nah, you drongo, he was never champ."

"Wasn't it Bob Fitzsimmons?" someone else queried.

"Nah, mate, he was a fuckin' Kiwi! Just lived here for a bit."

"You've got that wrong, sport. The bugger was Cornish!"

"Whadda you say, cobber? You over there in the dog collar?"

"Yeah, padre…"

Pastor Bob got up and walked over to them. "I'm sure you could tell me much more than I could tell you," he said. "But please let me buy you all a drink."

"Aw, *now* you're talkin'! Make room for the padre! Good on ya, mate!"

From that time on, Pastor Bob was hooked, no pun intended. He was floored. And down for the count. The history of Australian boxing became an obsession.

And then one night he was sitting at the bar with the regulars, and someone said: "If you *really* want the low down, padre, that guy sittin' in the back there might tell ya. But he won't. Bart Honey, 'is name is. Knows everythin' about the sport, like. But won't tell ya."

Pastor Bob hadn't noticed him before. He was indeed sitting in the back of the bar, in the shadows, wearing natty clothes and a fedora and with a large cigar in his mouth. He was nursing a pint of beer.

Bob walked over to him. "Can I buy you a drink?" he said.

"Yeah, sure. How about a triple scotch?"

"A triple scotch it is."

"And a cigar."

"And a cigar. Sure."

"I see you're a clergyman. Did you know that Sugar Ray Robinson – possibly the greatest boxer there ever was – dreamt he killed his next opponent in the ring and wanted to call off the fight? His promoters got a couple of ministers and a priest, if I remember, to tell Sugar Ray it was a just a dream and that he should go ahead with the fight. So what happened? He went into the ring and fought the fight and the other boxer died. What would you have told him if he'd asked you, padre?"

"Respect your dreams."

"Well, God bless you! I think I'll buy *you* a drink! Hey, a drink for the padre over here!"

"I hear you're an authority on boxing… A *writer* on the subject?"

"Yeah, that's right."

"So what are you going out here… out woop woop, as they say?"

"Hell, what are *you* doing here, in this dump?"

"Converting the indigenous, you could say…."

"OK, I'm here because I'm disillusioned…"

"Because…?"

"Well, for starters, everyone confuses me with Bert Sugar!"

"Who's Bert Sugar?"

"Bless you! Oh what the hell, Bert Sugar was a really famous boxing historian, and besides writing about boxing, like me, he even dressed like me and wore a hat like mine and smoked cigars like mine…."

"Did he do these things before you or after you?"

"Hey, enough of that, padre! Well, of course I'm sure he would have said he did all those things first. What the hell!" (*Sotto voce:*) "I met him once. Nice guy, actually. Quite a character. And yeah, I have to admit: he knew his stuff. Have to admit it! Just wish people wouldn't confuse us."

Bart took a drink.

"He's dead, but I still get confused with him! *Why, why, why!*"

Pastor Bob patted him on the arm. "I'm sorry", he said.

"You said that was *one* reason you were disillusioned," continued Pastor Bob.

"Cultural amnesia!"

"Yes?"

"All these young boxing writers, they don't know about Young Griffo or Les Darcy or Jimmy Carruthers!"

"So tell me… I mean, I've heard about them…."

"Well, they were the real kings of Australian boxing. Sure, there have been others, especially since… but they're the three classic figures, for me at least."

And so Bart talked and talked, and Pastor Bob listened. And they drank.

After a while, Bart nodded confidentially to Pastor Bob. "I heard what those morons over there said", he whispered. "I talk to people! Just not to the likes of *them*. And *of course* Young Griffo was world champion!" He put his head closer to Bob's. "I've even heard there's a film of Griffo winning the championship from Torpedo Billy Murphy, the Kiwi boxer! Not supposed to exist, but who knows? That would be the Holy Grail of Australian boxing!"

"Extraordinary! And you really think it does exist?"

Bart put a finger to the side of his nose and then winked.

"By the way," said Pastor Bob, "talking of cultural amnesia…"

"Which indeed we were, padre."

"Yes, well, I studied theology of course, but I was also interested in philosophy in my days of training for the ministry. Sometime in the 1990s there was some fuss about a book by an American philosopher, describing his travels around the world from a philosophical viewpoint. OK, fair enough. But another American philosopher…"

"Americans! Tell me about them! You have to hand it to a few of them, though… But look at what happened to Young Griffo: America was the ruin of him. Same thing with Les Darcy. Jimmy C never went there, wise man."

"OK, yes. Indeed. Well, I guess so. I mean, yes…. This other American claimed that there'd been nothing before like those philosophical travel pieces. He presumably didn't even know about Count Hermann Keyserling's *Travel Journal of a Philosopher*, published way back in the 1920s! Now, if *I* knew about it, how come a well known professional philosopher didn't?"

Bart Honey's eyes had glazed over. "Time to call it a night, padre!"

Pastor Bob got up to leave.

"Didn't see a car outside, except the regulars'?" Bart Honey said.

"Well, I don't actually have a car…"

"*Out here?*"

"Oh, it's not all that far, really."

"Would you like a lift?"

"A lift would be nice…"

"I would have thought you might have a motorbike. Or at least a bicycle."

"I do have a bicycle. I rig a sort of trailer to it when I go for supplies. I'd appreciate a lift, though. As long as you can put my bike on your roof rack?"

"Sure! Now we're talking! Come on out and climb in, padre."

Chapter 4:

Kingship

"We've always thought he was *odd*. He was never like most other humans – he genuinely *liked* us, for one thing."

"If he's a little... *crazy*, does that mean what he's been teaching us about Jesus Christ is also – well..."

"*Of course not!*" interrupted Mr Archie, in a tone that was unusual for him – almost harsh, one might say. "Next you'll be asking if belief in God is crazy. That would be utterly foolish!"

The others nodded in agreement.

"Besides," continued Mr Archie, "what's 'crazy' about helping wombats?"

"So now that he's gone..."

"He's left me in charge... as a sort of *king*," Mr Archie said. "I don't know what to think!"

The wombats went into a huddle.

"We've talked it over, and we do want you to be our king."

"Why me?"

"You're the biggest. And the wisest. Also, you have the best singing voice

– by far."

"And he can pick up a paperknife!" someone added.

"*Really?*" queried some of the younger wombats.

"Come with me," said Mr Archie. He waddled into the house, followed by the others, climbed up on a chair and picked up the paperknife.

"How on earth did you do that!" "That's unnatural!" "Weird! But great."

"YOU MUST BE OUR KING!" they chorused.

"I won't serve."

"But we'll appoint you, Mr Archie."

"I'll abdicate."

"You'll – ?"

"Step down."

"You're the wombat born to be king!"

Mr Archie sighed. "You've read too many books," he said.

"I suppose we should call you King Archie from now on?" asked one of the younger wombats.

"Of course! Of course!" chorused some of the elders.

"Oh, well. If you have to," said King Archie resignedly.

"Does that mean I'm a *queen?*" asked his wife, Gwen.

"Yes, I suppose it does, dear."

"Oooh, wait until I tell the kids!"

"You forget that our children are scattered around this region, my love. We haven't seen any of them since they left home."

"Oh, that's true! In my excitement I somehow forgot..."

Queen Gwen wasn't exactly a bark painting, as someone observed. But King Archie loved her dearly. "You look like an angel," he often said to her: not at all original, of course, but surely heartfelt.

Chapter 5:

Enter Young Griffo

Through a warp in time there enters our first contender, a Greek Australian known as Young Griffo.

Albert Griffiths. Not exactly a Greek name: one assumes either he or his parents changed the surname. If so, Young Griffo changed it again when he became a professional boxer.

Griffo was an alcoholic who loved bar room brawls, yet in the ring he was – drunk or sober – as skilful and clever a boxer as they come.

At first his claim to the championship was disputed: it was accepted in Australia and England, but not in the USA. Later on the Yanks gave in (as Griffo might perhaps have put it).

Not just bar room brawls. To give you an idea, he got into trouble with the law for stealing a jacket from one of his former managers. On another occasion, for running around naked in public.

Did he bother to train for fights? No. Not usually, anyway.

Yet he fought the very best of his time, including Joe Gans, George Dixon, Frank Erne, Jack McAuliffe, and so many others.

Amongst those he defeated were Young Peter Jackson, Ike Weir and Torpedo Billy Murphy: also some of the best you could find.

He may have fought over two hundred fights, from around 1886 to 1904.

Split. Smoke. Flame. A door opens, closes, opens again, closes again.

Homeless, for a while. Panhandling.

Then living in a single room, through an other's generosity – whose was it, and indeed why?

Then....

Pastor Bob told them about all this.

They were bemused at first.

Chapter 6:

Dealing With Wrong-Doers

"Aren't we supposed to right wrongs? Like the Knights of the Round Table?" asked Sir Kerry.

"As far as I can see," said King Archie, "they spent most of their time fighting, maiming and killing. As well as having you-know-what with the ladies."

Some of the females blushed beneath their fur.

"What's you-know-what?" a young wombat whispered to his immediate neighbour.

"Sex," the other youngster whispered back.

"Oh."

"But didn't they *sometimes* right wrongs?" insisted Sir Laurie. "Sir Launcelot, for instance. I sort of identify with him: we have similar names, for one thing."

"You're Laurence and he was Launcelot… it's not the same name," spoke up Sir Maurie.

"I said *similar*, not the same!" corrected Sir Laurie.

"Yes, yes," sighed King Archie. "Sir Launcelot was indeed good at righting wrongs … as was Sir Gareth."

"A good thing you're not like Sir Mordred," Sir Laurie said to Sir Maurie. "He was a false knight, and he betrayed his king."

"I'm *nothing* like him," rejoined Sir Maurie, indignantly.

"No offence!"

"I certainly don't identify with Kay the Senechal," said Sir Kerry. "He was something of an ill-speaking, bad-tempered jerk."

"You don't have to identify with him," sighed King Archie. "It's not even the same name."

"But it's similar."

"Yes, but not the *same*."

"At least no one here is called Percy."

"Yes, Perceval was an unfortunately ill-mannered, insensitive, uncouth and foolish youth," said King Archie.

"He did get better as he went along, though," ventured Sir Laurie. "And he saw the Grail!"

"Some say he even attained it," put in Sir Maurie.

"And Gawain saw it, too!" interjected one of the more intelligent youngsters.

"And so did Sir Launcelot!"

"What about Sir Galahad?"

"Now, now…," said King Archie.

"Yes, what about the Grail?" piped up Sir Garry.

"Ah, one thing at a time, please! Now, are there any wrongs we should be addressing ourselves to?"

"Surely you've heard about that wombat who was kicked to death… kicked over and over again… by a man, while the man's friends stood by, watching, laughing and egging him on."

"Was it a young wombat?" someone ventured.

"Then why didn't his mum try to help him?" Queen Gwen asked.

"Or was it an elderly, arthritic wombat?" someone else asked.

"No," said Sir Laurie, "I believe it was a mature wombat, but an especially gentle and friendly one. Stunned by the first kick, I doubt the poor thing had much chance at all."

"Yes, I had heard," said King Archie. "Shocking! Terrible! How horrible humans can be. Do we know who this man is?"

"I do," said Sir Kerry.

"Then," said King Archie, "we can deliver an anonymous note to the local police, can't we? I can write it."

"He *is* the local police," said Sir Kerry.

"Oh dear! Any suggestions about how else we might deal with this situation?"

"Do you think you could handle a paintbrush, King Archie?" asked Sir Maurie.

"I can indeed. Pastor Bob showed me how."

"How about if we paint on his house that he's a fat drunken sod who's so ugly he can only have it off with his chooks? No one would ever suspect it was us!"

"I've already snuck by his place under cover of dark," said Sir Kerry. "He's been decorating the outside and has paint cans and brushes all about."

"Excellent!"

"But why chickens?"

"Well, it suggests he's got a really tiny penis… which he probably has."

"That's terribly rude!" exclaimed King Archie. "Actually, I like it. How about if we make it: 'Drunken sod so ugly he can only fuck chooks'?"

"But that gets away from the tiny prick idea. What if we make it: 'Ugly drunken sod is a chook fucker if lucky'?" asked Sir Garry.

"Or: 'Lucky you, you ugly drunken sod, if you can fuck chooks'?" said Sir Laurie.

"Perhaps a little long-winded," said King Archie. "Any other suggestions?"

" 'Drink, you ugly sod, your chooks await you.'"

"Um, possibly not explicit enough?"

" 'Sad ugly drunk, fuck chooks if you can.'"

" 'Drunken ugly sod who wishes he could fuck chooks.'"

"How about: 'Ugly drunken chook-fucker-wannabe'?"

"Would he or his friends understand the word 'wannabe'?" queried King Archie. "After all, he's sure to be a thick redneck bastard."

Sir Maurie spoke up. "How about: 'Thicko fat redneck bastard with tiny penis can't even fuck chooks'?"

"A little wordy?"

" 'No chook fucking for teeny pricked thicko bastard'?"

" 'Drunken sod thicko's prick snubbed by chooks'?"

" 'Even the chooks laughed at sad drunken sod's teeny weenie'?"

"Personally, I'd vote for 'Drunken ugly sod who wishes he could fuck chooks'. My wife, um, queen, has summed it up nicely, I feel. Any objections?" asked King Archie.

Much head-nodding ensued.

"You *all* disagree?"

Much head-shaking ensued.

"Motion carried, then," said King Archie. He paused thoughtfully. "It's a good thing Pastor Bob left that book of dirty poems lying around..."

"Yes, limericks! By someone called Douglas. We picked up a few useful words from that filthy bugger!"

"*Pastor Bob?*"

"No, Douglas!"

"There were those other books as well... Why do you think a holy man like Pastor Bob read such stuff?"

"I suspect," said King Archie, "that he wanted to understand his fellow men a little better."

"Ah, yes!"

Chapter 6:

Whatever Happened to Pastor Bob?

"You clearly don't take orders gladly – or at all!"

"I'm sorry," said Pastor Bob. "I know I misled you. But I did use some of my own money on the project… towards acquiring the land, building the house and so on."

"I had doubts about this scheme of yours from the first. For a start, we don't usually set out to convert, like old-fashioned missionaries, at least not these days; we're more to do with letting people come to *us*. However, you said there was already a church there, meant especially for Aboriginal Australians. We know that wasn't true. But as there were Lutheran missions for the indigenous in South Australia that we knew about, set up by our German brethren, it didn't seem unlikely that there was something similar in Victoria, even if we hadn't heard of it before."

"I think there was at least one independent Christian mission in Victoria…."

"No doubt." He paused, and sighed. "How many Aboriginal Australians were in your congregation by the time you left?"

"None."

"*None? Not a one?*"

"I only ever encountered a handful. Most of them had been wise enough to leave the place to the whites… and to the animals. I did talk with the remaining few, but they'd had enough of white influence and were content with their own religion and culture."

"You didn't try to persuade them otherwise?"

"No: once I found out about what they believed and so forth, I just respected them."

"And the whites?"

"I rather enjoyed having a drink with a few of them, as they were interesting enough, but that's as far as it went. A man named Bart Honey was the most interesting. Most of them were far beyond any redemption, in my opinion."

"Not very Christian of you!"

"Perhaps. But then you never met them."

The Bishop cleared his throat. "So it is true, that you set out to convert… um, *wombats!* Small furry creatures that walk on all paws, eat grass, burrow in the ground, can't speak and presumably can't think."

"Not all of what you say is true. Some of them are quite large, they can be taught to speak, and they do think."

"Arrant nonsense, Bob! Whatever has happened to you, man? Did you have a breakdown or something?"

The Bishop looked steadily at Pastor Bob, who had declined to reply. He leaned closer. "Tell me, truthfully, Bob: was this always your intention? To convert wombats, I mean."

"No, no. It just sort of… happened."

"*It just happened?!*"

"You know… *gradually*."

The Bishop sat in silence for a while, thinking, and then he said:

"You've mentioned your drinking…"

"Yes?"

"Well, we *are* Lutherans, not Baptists. But try not to let it get out of hand, Bob."

Pastor Bob nodded.

"So I think we need to arrange for you to have some counselling. Something a little *different*. And then…"

Chapter 7:

Taking Action

King Archie and a group of his senior followers – Sir Laurie, Sir Garry, Sir Maurie and Sir Kerry – arrived at the policeman's house late at night. They were dismayed to see lighted windows and hear the loud voices of carousers.

They could only hide, listen and watch, and wait for their chance.

"That sheila was a two-pot screamer, a bit of a slag, too… yeah, more than a bit! Aw, mate, I had a million butterflies coming out of me arse! Fair dinkum, she screamed aw'right when I gave it to 'er!"

"More like a ten-pot screamer, the bloody alkie. She can really put the amber liquid away."

"Aw, can I have the slag's number, mate?" The voice was definitely that of the policeman, as Sir Kerry confirmed in a whisper.

Laughter.

"Ain't in the bloody phone book, cobber. She's even more out woop woop way than we are, only comes over now an' again. Anyway, you's married! Yer wife's asleep right here…"

"Yeah, well, sometimes I think I'd be better off with a boong!" the policeman replied. "Never should have married the uptight bitch."

"What's going on?" Sir Laurie whispered to King Archie.

"They're being nasty about their women folk. And about the black people."

"Why?"

"Because they're nasty! And stupid. Shush, they'll hear us!"

"Aw, a boong's better than a whingeing Pom, anyways. Struth, look what happened to Bill!"

"Yeah, that's right, he got hitched to that Pom slag, Sally. Ruin of 'im. We never see the sod now, 'cept at work!"

"Yeah, an' she's got a face like a koala's bum."

"I don't s'pose Bill cares about her bloody face! Bet he just wants a Donald whenever he feels like it."

"Aw, whatever else you might say, a bloke's got needs. An' you can't just spank the wallaby *all* the time. You gotta hunt the golden doughnut whenever you can."

"Never a truer word, sport!"

It went on like that for some time. But finally the revellers left or, in the policeman's case, headed for bed.

The wombats headed off too… into action, with paint cans and paintbrush. They nudged the cans along, prised them open as best they could, and King Archie did the rest….

Chapter 8:

From Pastor Bob's Notebooks

Who said that history is a nightmare we're trying to wake up from? Not Henry Ford, anyway. And most definitely not the Roman historians. The Cathars might have, but certainly not Simon de Montfort.

Nor my so-called counsellor.

What is self-remembering? What is that self, and why is it worth remembering?

I, I, I: that's what I'm supposed to wake to. Normally I'm merely sleep-walking, because when I eat a sandwich I don't remember that *I'm* eating the sandwich, or if I take a shit it's *me* doing the shitting. Only my counsellor doesn't use those particular examples.

Do I remember myself when I'm drinking? Moral application: rarely if ever considered the point of this sort of exercise.

When I say I taught wombats to read and speak English, do I remember myself in this act of talking about said wombats? Therapeutic application: seldom if ever considered the point, either.

When I celebrate the Eucharist, am I remembering myself in the act of celebration? Religious application: no, nor that.

So I have to admit he's taken an entirely miserable obsession with the self and tried to turn it into something a little... *different.* Still quite ridiculous, but, yes, different. I did ask him once if his original point of departure was Maurice Nicoll, however much he then diverged; he replied that it was not relevant to our concern with *self-remembering* to go into matters of intellectual origination. So be it.

And *this* is their idea of counselling!

Chapter 9:

Pastor Bob's Departure

It was the day before flying out of the country, and Pastor Bob was sitting over a glass of brandy at a bar.

A young Australian couple noticed him sitting alone and looking sad. "Let's go over and cheer the poor man up," said Shirley to her partner, Neil.

"Hello," said Shirley. "I see you're a minister. And we couldn't notice but that you're by yourself on a Friday night. My name's Shirley. This is Neil, my boyfriend. Can we join you?"

"Oh, of course," said Pastor Bob, wishing they wouldn't. "My name's Bob. Pastor Bob."

"So you're obviously a religious sort of person," said Neil. "Not my thing, I'm afraid. I'm a linguist. A research linguist. Shirley's a lexicographer, working on an online dictionary."

"Ah!" said Bob. "Language! That's my other main interest. In fact, I thought of becoming a linguist once myself." He mused: "Language is giving and sharing; dividing and distinguishing; affirming and denying – or negating; disclosing and relating. Relating to what we see and hear, disclosing, receiving…."

"But surely we do these things without language? We give things, we receive things, and so on…," said Shirley.

"Yes, yes. I agree! But that all plays into language, and language plays into all of it."

"Didn't someone say 'Language is the Throne of the Other'?" Neil asked. "Some French thinker I was reading about..."

"People say all sorts of daft things," replied Pastor Bob.

He paused.

Then he took a sip of his drink and leaned towards them. "I've been experimenting with teaching the English language to wombats. With remarkable success!"

Shirley and Neil looked at each other, and then both burst out laughing.

"That's *very* funny, Pastor Bob!" exclaimed Neil.

"Hilarious! You *are* quite a joker!" said Shirley.

Pastor Bob smiled wryly.

Chapter 10:

Reprisals (1)

When the policeman found out what the wombats had done, he was of course furious. And needless to say he didn't for a moment suspect the real culprits.

He gathered his friends together.

"I know who it must have been – those Poms who live over that way," he said pointing into the distance. "Never liked or trusted 'em! They're *different*... I mean, for starters, they're not real Aussies!"

"Aw, an' somehow the buggers are growin' their own veggies... *out here!* How the fuck are they doin' it? We have to buy 'em from the general store... and the store has to have them driven or even *flown* in."

"And raisin' their own sheep and cattle! While we're stuck workin' on the bloody sheep station."

"Ain't right! Ain't fair!"

"Let's teach those Pommy bastards a lesson!"

"Struth, yeah, one they won't forget in a bloody hurry!"

However, they not only picked on the wrong... *creatures*; they were also picking on the wrong sort of Poms.

It took some time, because there was coordination and planning involved, but they eventually found that the English family were away for a couple of nights, leaving only one of their boys in charge, and they took their chance.

They sneaked up behind the boy and knocked him unconscious. Then they smashed all the windows, and wrote in paint on the side of the house: "Fuck off home Pommy bastards!"

Unfortunately for him, the policeman couldn't resist also writing something in biro on the front door frame. It read: "Dont fuck with the police Poms!"

It would, as they say, come back to bite him.

They also stole sheep and cattle. That also would come back to bite them.

Chapter 11:

How Pastor Bob became a Chaplain, and What Happened Then

Pastor Bob wasn't burned at the stake: those times had thankfully passed; and Lutherans were not given to such things, anyway. Instead, he was... *removed* to a certain notorious English university, to be its chaplain.

I say "notorious", but in point of fact it was no worse than many another English university... things had become *that* bad by this time.

His spirits were crushed. As he knew, academic standards had fallen so badly that some graduates could barely spell or put a sentence together: certain of them couldn't, in fact, at all. (We're not talking about genuine cases of dyslexia here, rather laziness about learning basics. In Chaplain Bob's admittedly limited experience, genuinely dyslexic students tended to use what help they could get in order to get on: he would come to help the occasional one out himself.) Students asserted in exams that, for example, Virginia Woolf was a 1960s feminist, a friend of Germaine Greer and the founder of Bloomsbury Publishing. It was also said that Peter Shelley (yes, *Peter* Shelley, not even Percy, let alone Mary... much less Bram Stoker) wrote *Dracula*, whose "hero" was "an odd gentleman from overseas who couldn't fit in when he came to England as a refugee". These same students criticised, complained about and made demands of their lecturers in the name of "client satisfaction". And of course they received degrees.

Chaplain Bob took to the bottle: really and truly. He'd already been drinking when he was in Australia, as we've seen. And before. But this had been comparatively little at all. And he cried every night thinking of his beloved wombats.

Excessive drinking had a truly unfortunate effect on Chaplain Bob: from a gentle, quiet, affable and generous person, if something of a loner, he degenerated into a quarrelsome, tediously loquacious and bitter character.

Weirdly, he had recurrent nightmares about a performance artist who nailed his own penis and scrotum to a board. No such person existed, needless to say, Bob told himself.

One day a certain student presented himself at Chaplain Bob's office.

"Chaplain Bob," he said, "I've been wondering: how can you believe in God when God doesn't exist?"

"What do *you* believe in?" Bob snapped.

"Humanity. I believe in humanity."

"Tell that to surviving Concentration Camp victims or their families, or those of Stalin's gulags, or the survivors of Idi Amin's regime, or Salazar's, or Mao's, or Ceauşecu's, or Hoxha's, or Pinochet's."

"*Who? What?*"

Bob tried to enlighten him; he even talked about Clausewitz, he talked about Genghis Khan and Attila the Hun; he also mentioned Machiavelli, and touched on the Marquis de Sade and Gilles de Rais.

The youth sagged at his post.

"Yes," he ventured, "but why didn't God stop those people?"

"You think God is a being who should rain down thunderbolts on anyone he doesn't like?"

"Well, *yeah*..."

"Or perhaps that he shouldn't permit them to exist in the first place?"

"Well, *yeah*.... I mean, what about the Jews killed by the Nazis, as you just explained to me?"

"Where was God when the Nazis killed the Jews? The question fails itself: why did human beings do these things, in the face of God? Didn't God self-reveal in every Jew's face?"

"I don't think I understand.... Do you mean you can see God in every person's face? Mine, for instance?"

"*Let's not get carried away*," Pastor Bob said beneath his breath.

"What?"

"Oh, I need a drink." He shook his head and sighed. "Let's go back to what we were talking about before. What about all the contemporary killings in Palestine? They're still going on."

"Is there really such a place called that? I thought it was a made-up name!"

"Oh God! Oh God!" Chaplain Bob groaned.

"Are you all right?!"

"Oh, don't worry about me. By the way, what do you know about Virginia Woolf?" asked Chaplain Bob. "It's just a wild card question."

"Isn't that a play by some American, Edward Something-or-Other? I think we did it on the Modern American Drama module."

"You've read *Who's Afraid of Virginia Woolf?*"

"I haven't *read* it. We don't read anything: our lecturers do that for us."

"You don't read *at all?*"

"Well, there's the odd handout, never more than a page. The lecturers wouldn't get away with giving us anything longer than that! We'd *complain!*"

"I *really* need a drink."

"I could do with a drink myself. Any chance of buying me one, Chaplain Bob? The student bar's open."

A few drinks later… with awkward attempts at conversation…. With Chaplain Bob lonely and dispirited, and the student desirous of free booze.

"So you've never had… um, sex?" the student asked.

"What do you take me for? A Catholic priest? A monk? *A nun?*"

"Shouldn't you be… *married*, though?"

"Well, yes, of course. I *was* married. Before I became a minister. Perhaps I've just been unlucky. Perhaps I'm too much of a loner. And in the outback…"

He sighed.

"There *was* the local policeman's wife. Apparently he, the policeman I mean, had a tiny penis. As well as being an obnoxious bastard, which she should have realised before marrying him. He really put the 'rat' into 'ratbag'." He laughed. "I can't claim any originality for that last remark."

"Ratbag?"

"Oh, someone really stupid, foolish, you know…"

"So you had an *affair* with her?"

"Yes, yes. If that's what you want to call it."

"An *adulterous* affair?"

"Yes, if that's how you want to put it!" He leaned closer. "*If you spread this around…*"

"W-wouldn't ever!" He hurriedly finished his drink. "It's been fun talking to you, Chaplain Bob. Must run!"

Bob became even more morose.

Then a student left a flyer in front of him.

Chapter 12:

Koalas

One day a package was left by the postman at the Mission: addressed to King Archie (or rather, Mr Archie).

It was Chaplain Bob's own copy of *Sixpence to Spend*, inscribed "to my dear, dear wombat friend."

This must be a sign! thought King Archie.

King Archie cried.

But the story certainly doesn't end there.

There had been rumours for quite some time. About koalas, or even a single koala, visiting the Mission. Expectations.

"These could be descendants of the Tribe of Koala Elder Norm," said Sir Laurie.

"Who?" asked Sir Maurie.

"They're there! I've heard about them!"

"Weren't they all killed? In somewhere called Herne Bay?"

"No, not at all!"

"You don't mean that Norman Lindsay fellow?" someone queried.

"No, *of course* not! We're talking about a *koala*, remember?"

Cultural amnesia! Must one have to rehearse the plight of the Herne Bay koalas yet again?

Hopefully not.

One day a female koala did indeed present herself at the Mission.

"Ah! So many generations have passed. But here I am, descendent of Norm and Doreen, and the heir to Koala Wisdom."

"And your name, please?"

"Earleen. Earleen the Koala."

"*Earleen?* What sort of name is that?"

"It's *my* name. And, by the way, what sort of name is *Archie?* For I believe that's *your* name."

"Pastor Bob gave it to me. It's a perfectly acceptable name for a wombat, as he assured me."

"Ah! Mine was given to me by my parents."

"And so – ?"

"Was this Pastor Bob a holy man, as I hear tell?"

"The holiest!"

"Then I salute you! Your lineage, though less direct than my own, is clearly of the highest."

King Archie made a slight bow, more like a nod really. Earleen did the same.

"I think I might be of service to your Highness," said Earleen.

"Does your lineage permit this?" asked King Archie.

"Ah yes."

She dipped into a small bag around her upper body. "I need to eat," she said. "These leaves don't keep too well once they've been plucked. I've had to stop off several times on my way here."

"You could eat with us, if you like," said King Archie while she nibbled.

"What's on the menu?"

"Grass. Scrub."

"Ah no, we koalas are gourmets. We only eat eucalyptus leaves."

"I see. I'd heard something to that effect."

"Now, we need to talk," said Earleen. "Before I can help you..."

"To...?"

"Don't you know? Aren't you looking for something?"

"And *you're* here...?"

"Because of spirit dreams, of course. I've dreamt of you, I've dreamt of your quest. As the principal heir to Koala Wisdom, I felt I should come and help if I could... *and* if advisable, of course."

"Hmmm. So Koala Wisdom came about through a koala named Norm?

That's what we've heard, anyway. But then there was the *event*... when koalas were captured and sent to somewhere in England called Herne Bay as convicts, in a misguided attempt to assist in producing eucalyptus oil for all sorts of remedies and so forth..."

"Norm the Wise, the Great Koala Elder. Well, he disseminated Koala Wisdom, at any rate. And taught us to speak and write, as well. When he arrived back in Australia, he regathered his tribe, and married a koala named Doreen, who had formerly been the partner of another koala, named David. We don't believe David survived his time in Herne Bay."

"And can you explain Koala Wisdom to me? In a sentence?"

She made a sound a little like a chuckle. "Can you sum up your faith in a sentence?"

"Jesus Christ died and rose again for our sake."

"I see. And is that it?"

"No, of course not!"

"I see. And you expect me to sum up Koala Wisdom in a sentence?"

"You might try."

"I don't think you'd really understand. Let's say it's about, first and foremost, belief and trust in the Great Spirit Koala. Then about how opposites are inadequate, how the direct seeing of individual things or animals is of primary importance, as is what we call 'branches,' by which we move from one thing to another and to another and finally to the Great Spirit Koala, and how transcendence is *utterly* important. There's a lot more, however. To do with contemplation and with spirit dreams."

"Are there any koala writings?" asked King Archie. His head was swimming but he didn't wish to say so.

"Not to do with the Wisdom tradition. Norm tried telling a couple of Englishmen about it once, and at least one of them was a writer, but neither were interested. Apparently David the Koala left a Captivity Narrative, scratched into bark. The last time a koala tried his hand, or rather, paw, at writing, it was stolen from him – in as much as it was changed and then published under another name. Not only that, it was supposed to be a hoax."

"They said it was a hoax that a koala had written it?"

"No, no. Ed wasn't even mentioned. They claimed it was written by a recently deceased garage mechanic and watch repairman, and then they 'revealed' that they'd written it themselves as a sort of joke. It was supposed to show how foolish the people were who'd taken it seriously."

She paused.

"The original title was *The Darkening Eucalyptus*. They changed that, as they changed much else. But what they presented to the world was very much based on Ed's writing."

"How did Ed the Koala get the manuscript to them? And why?"

"He didn't get it to them. Keith did."

"Who's *Keith*?"

"Keith the Koala. Ed's older brother. He delivered it to one of those people… left it on the doorstep with a little note. A bundle of scratched leaves and pieces of bark at a time. As a favour to Ed. Poor Ed thought he was giving something valuable to the world."

"But… but… what about the Holy Grail? If you're really here to help us, as you say, you must know about it. Pastor Bob says it's a film! And we're supposed to find it."

"A *film?*"

"Yes, well, I thought it was a *cup* – a cup that Christ's blood was collected in. But apparently it's an old film."

"I know of films *about* the Holy Grail. Let's see, there's *The Light in the Dark*, that's an early film, and apparently quite good. It has an actor named Lon Chaney in it. And much more recently, there's something called *The Fisher King*. That's good as well, or so I hear."

"How on earth do you know this sort of stuff?"

Earleen gave him a Mata Hari look, secretive and… *knowing.* "I get around," she said.

"It might also be seen as the basis for the Communion of Saints. Not only was Christ's blood collected in it, it was also used to drink from at the Last Supper," said King Archie, summoning up his last reserves of imparted knowledge from Pastor Bob.

"Ah! We have what's known as the Communion of Koalas in *our* teachings," Earleen said.

King Archie groaned. This was getting far too complicated.

"By the way," Earleen suddenly said, "the cup *glowed.*"

"Sorry? What?"

"The cup. The chalice. The Grail. In *The Light in the Dark*. And besides, I've seen it."

King Archie looked puzzled. "You've seen it?"

"Ah, I'm afraid I can't tell you any more."

"But I'm a king!"

She smiled sadly and touched his paw with her own. "I know, dear. But even kings have their limitations. I can't tell you why, but you haven't passed the test. Bye!"

"*But… but….!*"

She turned and looked over at him. "Ooh, I see now. A copy of *Sixpence to Spend*. A great book. And also a collector's item, by the way. What a find!"

"It's mine! A present! And I hope you're not going to tell me it was really written by a koala?"

She looked at him askance. "Don't be silly!"

"*Although our knowledge of our soul is not complete, what we do know of it through consciousness or inner sensation is enough to demonstrate its immortality, spirituality, freedom, and several other attributes we need to know. And this seems to be why God does not cause us to know the soul, as He causes us to know bodies, through its idea. The knowledge that we have of our soul through consciousness is imperfect, granted, but it is not false,*" quoted King Archie, rather desperately.

"You'll be quoting Maine de Biran to me next!"

"No way! But you'll probably be quoting Fabre d'Olivet!"

"Not a chance! Bye bye!"

Chapter 13:

Performance

Why Chaplain Bob went along to the performance was anybody's guess… at any rate, he certainly didn't know. A combination of boredom and curiosity? Probably.

He was ushered into a small room. Fortunately there was a makeshift bar at the back. He ordered a drink and then found a seat.

The lights went down and then up again.

A soprano saxophonist played rather rambling free improvisations, while someone pranced about, exclaiming over and over: "I've got his coat! I've got his coat! The great musician! *His* coat – I'm wearing it!" Finally another voice pronounced: "He was *the* English improvising sax player who sounded like a busker and sometimes was!"

The lights went out, to a smattering of applause.

Then the lights went on again.

Chaplain Bob noticed that the young man sitting next to him was blushing and visibly agitated. He had a snazzy jacket on. He made for the door in what was clearly a temper.

"Rather cruel," thought Bob.

The lights went down, and up again.

This time someone screamed and shouted into an acoustic guitar until he was hoarse and red-faced, but continued as best he could. His fellow performer wore a gas mask, and wove drunkenly between the members of the audience, eventually standing in front of Chaplain Bob. "You! *She* who's in the frock!" he shouted out, after removing the mask, to some uneasy laughter, and moving away again.

"Well, I *am* wearing robes," Chaplain Bob thought to himself. "Just the same.... Let's say I was a wombat! What would I do?"

He went over to the now unmasked student performer and tipped the remainder of his drink over the young man's head.

"Wow!" someone murmured. "Audience participation: and from Chaplain Bob...."

The ersatz guitarist shouted into his instrument.

Applause. Again the lights were lowered and then raised.

Chaplain Bob returned his glass to the makeshift bar.

"Don't go now, Chaplain Bob! This is going to be the best part of the show. I think you'll really be surprised."

"OK, then give me another drink."

"Another drink coming right up!"

Again the lights were lowered, and then went up again.

Two students, one male and the other female, were sitting on chairs. A small, mixed group of figures stood to one side of them.

WIFE *(talking into her mobile)*: Is this the gas company? Yes?

HUSBAND: Do we have a leak or something?

WIFE *(to husband)*: No, no, dear.... *Shush....* *(speaking into the mobile:)* No, no, I was just speaking to my husband. Now, I have this leaflet here that says you're asking for volunteers from the general public to appear in your annual play. Is that right? Yes? Well, what parts are left? A fairy and an angel? We don't believe in fairies. But I think my husband would do a good job of the angel.

HUSBAND: *Me? Why me?* Anyway, I'm not sure I believe in angels!

WIFE *(to husband)*: *Shush, dear....* *(speaking into mobile:)* No, not you, I was speaking to my husband again. So, when and where is the audition? Wait a minute, I'll just write that down. *(She writes in a notepad.)* Yes, don't worry, he'll be there! Goodbye.

HUSBAND: You might have asked me!

WIFE: Oh, I think it will be fun. You know, I've wondered about writing a play about angels myself. How they feel, how they make ethical decisions, those sort of things.... Do they have and do these things much the same as we have and do, or is there some... special light in which they exist and move and act?

HUSBAND: Perhaps they're more like automata, with no feelings or ability to form decisions. Perhaps they just act according to the will of God without any input of their own.

WIFE: You don't think highly sophisticated robots might be able to have feelings or make decisions of their own?

HUSBAND: They'd be implanted in them, as simulations.

WIFE: Well, why don't we ask those angels standing over there?

HUSBAND: *What? Where?*

The first angel comes forward.

FIRST ANGEL: We've heard what you've been saying about angels, and I'm afraid it means nothing to us. *Utterly* beside the point. We've talked it over… quietly, of course. You wouldn't have heard.

The first angel moves away.

The second angel moves forward. She looks steadily at the husband but remains silent, and then also moves away.

The third angel moves forward. He too looks steadily at the husband, in silence. But then he raises his arms so that his fists touch and his forearms form a straight line. He does this slowly, but then he suddenly and violently pushes them away from his chest, in the direction of the husband (though without touching him).

The husband falls off his chair. His wife leans down and searches for a pulse, then shakes her head.

WIFE: Ah, too bad! I rather liked him. He wasn't a bad husband at all.

The fourth and last angel moves forward. He's built like a football player, or possibly a boxer. He reaches down and grabs the husband's arms, and pulls him up onto the chair. Then he moves away.

HUSBAND: What a weird experience!

WIFE: How do you feel, dear?

HUSBAND: I feel like I want to play that angel in the gas company's performance.

WIFE: Ah, how nice....

*

The lights went out, and then on again. The actors bowed to the audience. Applause, some of it hesitant, and some embarrassed coughs and half-suppressed laughs. Puzzled looks from some. A young man in the audience stood up and gave a wave: the playwright, Chaplain Bob surmised; he made his way over to the bartender, and they hugged. Bob would have liked to have talked with him, but didn't feel that he could, not at that time. He got up and hurried to the door, and then found his way out of the building and then away from the university; his vision was blurred, less by alcohol than by emotion.

He kept going, heading for home.

"But it's come too late," he concluded sadly. He began to sob. Then cried uncontrollably. "I can't change now!"

Chapter 14:

Enter Les Darcy

Through another warp in time, our second contestant, Les Darcy, enters.

We do have films of Darcy. Not very good in quality, *but even so*.... Films, just the same. Hard on the eye.

Darcy was a former blacksmith, like Bob Fitzsimmons. But like another great boxer, Mexican Joe Rivers, he also played the violin. Go figure.

He was much loved in the local community in Maitland, New South Wales, and loved his family, providing for them from his earnings; he was a church-goer, too. Other boxers were known to respect him and even give him gifts as remembrances.

He fought in a swarming, full-on, aggressive way... *courageous*. Aggressive? Yes. But not with any malice, or vicious spirit: a desire to win, but not by any means a murderous desire. With *heart*, you might say, and some say he died of a broken heart when he was accused of being a coward for not enlisting as a soldier in the First World War.

He'd defeated Jeff Smith, George Chip and George "K. O." Brown, amongst many others. In Australia he was regarded as the World Middleweight Champion, but the Yanks, as Bart Honey might say, refused to acknowledge him.

He died of infected teeth. He was 21 years old.

An image can be torn; a wall can of course collapse; a skull can be cracked;

a mind can become battered even pulverised, or else distempered, ensnared by all manner of falsehood and delusion; but can a heart be broken? Yes.

Chapter 15:

From Chaplain Bob's Notebooks

God allows himself to be killed all the time. That's the meaning of Creation, and of the Crucifixion. Himself? A mere convention to speak in this way. "He," I mean. A convention, or surely to be taken as such.

Die, at any rate.

To rise again.

. . . .

Predestination and so-called hard determinism are like solipsism: you can neither prove nor disprove them rationally, but they hardly make much sense. Only religious fanatics, philosophers or mad people subscribe to such.

. . . .

Is religion the new atheism? When religion held sway, atheism was a counter-force. But now that atheism largely holds sway...? But I'm being flippant, even as I try not to be.

Perhaps one should say that dogmatic atheists are the mirror image of dogmatic, fundamentalist Christians: profoundly limited in their vision of things, incapable of serious dialogue, smug... *self-righteous*. An atheist once said to me: Atheists like Richard Dawkins give atheism a bad name. And if Christianity has, wrongly, disgracefully, dreadfully done much in its past to punish those who believe *differently*, so have atheist regimes... and pagan cultures. No use making excuses: when Constantine embraced Christianity, he did much for the Christian church and much against the Christian faith, falsely allying it with secular power. Dogmatism, intolerance and sectarianism did the rest, not to mention vicious fanaticism.

Could killing God... or attempting to do so... be an affirmation of God? Is denying the very possibility of God a denial of possibility? And thus perhaps a negation of itself? And leading to further negations?

A denial of the entire basis of possibility, which is infinity? If we can imagine an infinity of possibilities, does that include God or indeed is it because of God? And is that infinity of possibilities based on what there is physically, as well as what we feel and what we see in dreams and visions? Or could it be that it precedes all that?

But I myself have written, "God allows himself to be killed all the time. That's the meaning of Creation, and of the Crucifixion. *Die*, at any rate." Doesn't that mean that an infinity of possibilities is not the same *sense* of infinity as when we speak of God's infinity? Just as eternity doesn't simply – simply? – mean an endlessness of time? Nor the opposite of time. Rather a rupture and illumination.

Infinity isn't what we can count until we can't count any more.... That's a dim reflection at best. It's what's beyond any counting or any total sum of things. Reflection? Yes, what can be reflected *within* the world but never part of the world, never a thing in the world or the world itself.

So does that mean it's not a matter of what we see or sense until we can't see or sense any more....

Timelessness isn't a frozen segment of time. It's not part of time at all, nor its opposite. It makes itself manifest through time.

When Lazarus was raised from the dead, he *reeked*; when Jesus Christ rose again, there was no odour of death, nor would there ever be.

Eternity and infinity are the abstract expressions of God. Love and compassion are the concrete expressions.

But if we are in darkness and pain... why then doesn't God self-reveal?

God isn't a god (or goddess). So necessary to repeat this and keep on repeating it. A god is a being amongst other beings, such as a person, a dog or a fly, only with different abilities or powers. Does this mean we should dismiss or denigrate all accounts of gods... or spirits? I don't believe so. Such accounts do tell us something, especially in the more purely supernatural aspects.

Surely God does self-reveal. Continually. But we are blinded by our own interventions, our own actions, our own inventions.

Eternal life isn't just a matter of glimpsing the eternal, as we may do here and now, but living in it and indeed living it. Some may feel they are doing this now, in this present life, and not just in glimpses or in dark reflection. If so, so: God has blessed them more than I've been blessed. But I wonder....

Chapter 16:

Reprisals (2)

The English settlers were racist – they hated blacks; and were also anti-Semitic. But they believed in animal rights, oddly enough, and had been appalled when they heard about how the policeman had kicked a wombat to death.

And then their house was trashed and their animals stolen.

They had gone round to see some of the policeman's friends and found their pilfered sheep and cattle. They'd had suspicions, and the suspicions were justified. They dealt mercilessly with the perpetrators.

And they were led, without any doubt on their part, to the policeman's house. He was there with the remainder of his cronies. His wife, fortunately for her, was visiting her mother in faraway Wooloomooloo.

"We don't mind if you beat up or even kill a few blacks – we came out here to get away from their sort – "

"Well, you picked the wrong bloody place, didn't you, you stupid fucks?"

"All right, we didn't do our homework, true enough; we *have* driven most of them away, however. But kicking a poor animal to death just isn't on. Yes, we heard about that wombat you killed. And now you turn on us!"

"Who are you to tell us what to flaming do, sport?"

"We're not here to tell you anything, *sport*. We're here to teach you a lesson.

You. Plain and simple."

"What the fuck?! Where do you Poms get off even talkin' to us like that."

"You've brought it on yourselves."

The fight that ensued was brutal, to say the least. Barbaric? Yes.

In the end, only the policeman was left alive. Or so he thought.

Chapter 17:

Chaplain Bob Writes to King Archie at the Mission

My dear Wombat Friend,

Jesus comes back from the dead, but not as a dead man revived. He isn't recognised at first – he is the same yet not the same. He is just someone, it seems. And then he is recognised. As the Christ.

In the 'Gospels' what happens is that the disciples encounter a reality and a personhood – a sense of what a person might be – that surpasses anything they've ever experienced before, and which challenges them to the core. What is this? It's resurrection; it's the overcoming of death. How? Where? In an afterlife. An afterlife we all can enter, if only we have faith. The Resurrection is a revelation – of eternal life, of life that transcends death. The story of the encounter on the road to Emmaus, for example, is a revelation. These stories speak of what could not have been spoken or written in any other way.

The temptation to see Christ as a god, alongside Greek and Roman gods, was stumped by the Crucifixion. How could a god be – let himself be – executed like a common criminal? Yet the Resurrection was even more of a stumbling block.

Does it point to absence where one expected presence, and presence where one expected absence?

But I have something else to tell you... about the Grail!

246

Of course! How can I have been so stupid! It's at Bart Honey's! *He misled me...* *yet also told me at the same time.*

With love,

Bob

(Your Former Pastor in Christ)

Chapter 18:

The End of Chaplain Bob

The final stage of Chaplain Bob's decline was rapid. He became increasingly belligerent. He often refused to turn up at the university, and spent his time sleeping all day and drinking and watching old films on his laptop during the night. On the rare occasion when he did manage to wander into college, he was drunk and either it was so late that the building was closed, or else no students wanted to see him, rather unsurprisingly.

He never got to talk to the student playwright, who'd dropped out of the university almost immediately after the performance of his short play. Chaplain Bob wasn't surprised: what, he thought, was a kid like that doing in a place like this, anyway?

He and the Head of English had quarrels whenever they met or, more regularly, sent each other messages. Bob precipitated the exchanges. Usually very late at night or early in the morning. Bob accused him of encouraging illiteracy and of being a toady, a blockhead and... well, it got worse and worse.

Eventually Bob was fired after referring to the Provost and Chancellor as "ignorant, sell-out gobsuckers" at one of the extremely few public gatherings he attended that had to do with the university. Actually, what he said was either misheard or deliberately misreported: "gobsucker" wasn't really the word he used. And what he said about the Head of English was strictly unprintable, but had something to do with mothers, backsides and mucus.

He died soon afterwards.

No foul play was suspected.

His books and papers were destroyed. Many volumes of theology, novels by Natsume Sōseki, Mark Twain, Charles Williams, Bernard Malamud and others, and numerous notebooks. All consigned to the flames.

Chapter 19:

Reprisals (3)

The English settlers' place was torched. But in the fight before, there'd been heavy losses on both sides.

The policeman guarded the doors and windows, just in case. His friends had all been killed.

But the others....

He thought he and his buddies had killed them all.

He was wrong.

One of the Poms survived. There was a secret exit, under the floorboards. And the Pom was out for revenge.

Chapter 20:

Le Morte d'Archie

"More Poms!" thought the policeman as he staggered over to the Mission, armed with kerosene, rags and matches. "A Pom set this up. More Poms will follow, even if he's gone. I'll torch the place!"

He didn't get a chance.

King Archie was waiting, holding his paperknife. He suddenly burst into song – his death song. A rich tenor voice, a strong melody....

> *a lion yes*
> *perhaps yes*
> *if a wombat*
> *might be a lion*

> *a lion yes*
> *perhaps yes*
> *if a wombat*
> *might be a lion*

> ***a lion yes***
> ***perhaps yes***
> ***if a wombat***
> ***might be a lion***

"*What the hell?*" the policeman and one other cried out as one. For he'd been followed. And his assailant, despite his shock, struck out. The blow that felled the policeman would almost have been enough to kill him instantaneously. But he was still just alive, only *just*, when he landed on something on the floor: something, or someone, *singing*.

His fall was sufficiently heavy to kill King Archie, crushing the poor wombat. However, it also contributed to his own death: for he fell on King Archie's clenched paperknife, sufficiently sharp to pierce his heart.

"I've pierced his foul heart," thought King Archie as he expired.

So did the foul-hearted policeman expire as well.

More wombats were waiting. Many more.

Sir Maurie kicked the assailant with his back legs and, as the assailant started to fall, he went for his shins.

The others finished the job. They moved with a speed that belied their ordinarily indolent nature, and they put aside all their ordinary gentleness. You could say: *they'd had enough*. Teeth, claws, back legs.

Unfortunately, the person they were attacking wasn't their enemy at all. As one of them realised straight away.

"No! No!" called Sir Garry. "He attacked our real enemy, the policeman… and it wasn't his fault our enemy fell on King Archie."

But he was ignored, due to the blind rage of his fellows.

And when, with thought, the others eventually realised their mistake, they grieved.

But they grieved even more for their dead and beloved king.

In sorrow, they abandoned the Mission.

They dispersed.

Chapter 21:

Enter Jimmy Carruthers

Through yet another warp in time, enter Jimmy Carruthers: our third contestant, or, you might say, contender… or even claimant.

Carruthers fought with distinction as an amateur, and was undefeated as a professional from 1950 to 1954, when he retired.

As was said and, we believe, truly so, Jimmy Carruthers was a gentleman, inside and outside of the ring. In his second fight with Vic Toweel, whose bantamweight championship he'd annexed in a single round, rushing the South African boxer from the bell and pummelling him to the canvas, Carruthers wore Toweel down and eventually knocked him out; as soon as the defeated man had been counted out, the Australian rushed to him: in solicitude, we might say; and rightly, I think.

That was his first defence. He later successfully defended his championship against Henry "Pappy" Gault, and then against Chamroen Songkitrat in Bangkok in an open air ring during the monsoon season, fighting in bare feet and having to wait from time to time for the apron to be cleared of debris.

Unlike Young Griffo, who if he'd kept any of his money might have opened a saloon, Carruthers opened a chain of juice bars back in Australia, as well as having interests in the hotel business and in vegetarian takeaway. But only after having to go back in the ring after his initial retirement, fighting when he was past his peak and for the first time losing. Learn a trade, he advised young boxers: boxing was the only thing I knew how to do, and I had to go back to it when I shouldn't have.

But I paraphrase....

There are indeed films of Carruthers fighting Vic Toweel, yes, both matches, as well as his fight with Chamroen Songkitrat. They're scarcely easier on the eye to watch than the films of Les Darcy. However, his expertise and athleticism are both obvious, as well as his strength and grace.

Prismatic. Prismatic? Yes, prismatic.

Refracted.

Chapter 22:

At Bart Honey's

"Welcome!" said Bart Honey.

He was clearly very drunk to call out a greeting to a wombat who'd entered his house.

The wombat in question was Sir Laurie.

Bart was watching an old film, silent, grainy and somewhat blurry, on a home projector with a sheet for a makeshift screen. Two men were boxing in the film.

"Yes, it's Young Griffo! Fighting Torpedo Billy Murphy. This isn't supposed to exist, you realise. Hah! Sorry... of course you don't!"

"It's the Holy Grail!" exclaimed Sir Laurie.

Bart Honey keeled over of a heart attack and died instantly.

The door blew shut. Sir Laurie tried his best to batter it down, but couldn't. Nor could he burrow under the stone floor.

He searched the kitchen but found nothing he was able to eat.

The film stuck in the projector and burst into flame.

"Ah well," Sir Laurie said to himself, "I've done everything I could. And it hasn't been a bad life: not in the least. I've done what any wombat would be proud of, surely."

He lay down to die. Resignedly. To die... slowly.

Chapter 23:

What Next Happened to Bob?

I'd said goodbye to an old friend – could it somehow have been my old friend Mr Archie? – after a long night of drinking. If it was him, I'd have been the only one who'd been at the grape. I wandered on and on in search of other places to find another drink... and eventually realised I'd missed the last train. But I walked and walked towards the train station, as that seemed somehow a good idea.... I walked and I walked, there were shops and stalls and even the odd outdoor cinema with just a few people crowded together to watch, but not any wine, and however long I walked, no train station, and then there were farm lands and then wilderness, and I turned back, and the same stalls and shops.....

Then there was a music shop, I used to buy recordings there....

A woman wearing a head scarf asked me if I'd buy her a meal. I said I'd buy her a drink, at least. We entered a bar and sat down. Finally: a bar! She removed her scarf. She was incredibly attractive. But then an old friend entered the bar – not Mr Archie, surely? I found myself buying two large bottles of wine and putting them in a bag. And I was back – back? – at a house where I seemed to reside. I found I had to share a room with a woman and her boyfriend. She confided in me that her vagina was so tight it hurt if someone penetrated her with his penis. I hoped her boyfriend was sympathetic. Did I say so? No. I was outside again looking for wine in a Chinese market and it was extremely late yet so many shops, stalls and cafés were open.

Then there were other houses where I thought I once lived.... I was able to go in... but no one knew me there, nor did I know them....

258

Then there were houses. Other houses, I mean.

One Christmas... I remember... or was it possibly New Year? Which I spent in a friend's flat while she was away.... Late in the evening I made a stir fry, hot oil of course in a pan, sausages, peppers, onions, mushrooms, rice with egg, garlic, ginger, pepper and salt. In the flat across from me someone had a barbecue on the landing. I was lost, but not too lost... then....

Of course he didn't realise he was dead.

The library is due to close for the night in an hour's time. I should have been there before this: I'm one of the members of the shift. But I can still go and help out. It's at the top of a spiral staircase. Difficult to get to. But I do.

No, they don't want me there. I even try to check out a book, but they won't allow me to. Even though I work there myself? I want that book! It means... I'm not sure what. I'm really not sure.

They really don't like me. I'm not sure I like them. Some of them, anyway.

Then I realise that they don't even see me. Don't see me – at all! Let me check out a book? I'm not there, as far as they can tell! No wonder they ignore me....

He began to realise something was seriously... amiss.

Did these things happen in the past? Or are they happening now? I'm confused....

He was distracted by a play of shadows. Play? Performance, perhaps. Distracted? Held, one might say. Shadows, none the less. But what sort of shadows? And of whom?

Not just shadows. There were people there, but I only saw their shadows. They were there, though, I sensed it somehow. Three of them, boxing in turns. Somehow

259

just their shadows. Yet as I say, people. There was skill... and joy... *laughter at each other's skill, in appreciation, and joy at it. One was a middleweight, another was a lightweight, and the third was a bantamweight. But it didn't seem to matter. Now that I've passed them and am continuing on, it doesn't matter at all to me, either.*

cold night rain
a stopper for the bottle of wine

stops

cold night radio
or orchids

in full bloom

lilies in full bloom

a lion an antelope says
or yes an antelope
the lion says an antelope
& yawns & sleeps

indeed ah yes
or a dear wombat

oh for dark glasses
my eyes my poor dear eyes

there were people
there were animals

people? animals?

ah yes I have the glasses now
yet how? or indeed... yes

or have I? have I the need of?
or had the light been eclipsed?
in some benediction?

yes perhaps

To pass from one embodiment to another.... If we are always embodied, and I think that must be true, does this mean that personhood somehow goes beyond embodiment, while always embodied just the same?

Was the Resurrection a reconfiguration, in which nothing was the same afterwards?

I follow a path that leads to the sea... but I am able to go around, around where the sea begins, and find myself in a garden where koalas dwell, alongside many other animals, sloths, pangolins, orang-utans, gorillas, even lions with their mates and their cubs, the cubs playing with the lions' tails but without incident... all of it without incident... people passing by, not just me but many others... all without incident....

Do I see two wombats coming towards me? Not from the sea, but from further inland.

Yes! And of course I know them!

Chapter 24:

What Happened to Archie Next?

Mr Archie awoke from a strange dream in which he'd been a king. He couldn't quite understand it.

Black. Black on blue. Stripes or... lines... some of them waving. Changing to green and greenish brown, on... blue... or white. Waving or wavering. Flickering? Ah, then everything white. Then black. Then thicker bands of green and greenish brown... bands?... stripes... or lines. They fluctuate, sometimes one thing, sometimes another. Darker? Lighter? One, then the other. On blue, or on white.

I'm on someone's lap, and he's stroking the fur on my stomach. Surely it's Pastor Bob?

He seems to have gone away, but surely he'll be back.

Of course he didn't realise he was dead.

"Do you still rule us?" someone asked. Was it possibly Laurie?

"No, no, I never have, not really, and definitely not now! But I love you all, especially you, Gwen, my angel...."

A host... a wisdom... of wombats seemed to hover around him, then they faded, and disappeared.

Had they really been there? 'Really?'

He was sure they had.

I thought I'd died. I hadn't at all: of course I hadn't. Pastor Bob did indeed stroke my stomach, as I sat on his lap. Gwen beckoned to me, as if to say she'd be with us soon: Pastor Bob and I. And then I saw Laurie, dear Laurie! "It didn't just glow," he said, "it burst into flame. It was beautiful. It was simply beautiful. And in those flames I saw something about kingship…."

Ah, I said, we are together, and will remain together. And more of us will follow.

Pastor Bob is here, of course he is, and he just said something about the parousia. I should know that word, but I'll have to ask him…. He knows so much. Is it fullness he means? But for now… yes, for now….

Ah, he says it's Jesus Christ's arrival, and that this is not just fullness, but an overflowing.

Arrival? What can he mean, I wonder?

Dear Jesus Christ, keep us in your arms as we keep you!

Enfolding… enfolding us… enfolded… enfolding….

And yes… unfolding….

A Koala Rhapsody

In the beginning was fur, and fur was good.

Eventually other things appeared, some good, some bad.

Eucalyptus leaves were good.

Fire was bad. So were human beings... for the most part.

Koalas realised they were the summit of creation. They were furry. And they were wise.

They believed in the Great Spirit Koala. And the Great Spirit Koala blessed them with wisdom.

But the Great Spirit Koala didn't always protect them from fire or from human beings.

They also got ill. And they aged and died.

Why?

These things were what followed on from the absolute purity and beauty of fur.

If only fur existed, nothing else would. Not even koalas. Koalas were the most perfect manifestation of fur. But once they became manifest, they were subject to all that was outside the *absolutely* perfect.

That included disease, peril, suffering, death.

Why?

Because koalas needed to make choices, not to be perfect in a false sense: of being like robots. I've heard of robots. They're made by humans, they're sometimes like humans, but they're not humans.

Humans are bad enough.

But once you're in a world where you make choices, then mistakes and dangers appear. And all sorts of possibilities. Some good, some bad. Couldn't all the possibilities be good possibilities? If you only ever choose what's good, and that's because you can't do otherwise, then you've been limited in your range of choices. Yeah.

But why all the diseases and suffering? Would a world where those things weren't possibilities be better?

All koalas could live forever, not age, not suffer, not get ill.

There'd be no room for more koalas! (Though now, mind you, there are too few of us.)

But what about the bad things... fire, and human beings?

If those things didn't exist, would koalas be in no danger? Would they exist perfectly for ever?

No, not perfectly, and not for ever. That's not how this existence is. And if it was, there would be other problems. As we've seen. Oh yeah.

But couldn't the Great Spirit Koala have prevented fire and human beings from existing?

Is fire always bad? Are human beings always bad?

Even if they're not, perhaps it would have been better if they hadn't come into being.

Koalas could sleep more easily.

Sometimes you've got to wonder

Pity that human beings never become wise, either.

But what if koalas never became ill, never got injured, never had to put up with all the boomerangs and slingshots of outrageous fortune? We could still die, but peacefully and painlessly.

We wouldn't take over the earth. It's not in our nature.

I suppose it's just how these things are, mate. Otherwise we'd be in Heaven, not on earth.

And I don't suppose you believe in Heaven, do you, mate?

We do.

We're wise.

Notes:

Beyond the Mirror of the Fatal Shore

This is Norman's true story, although I am not at liberty to reveal my sources, except to acknowledge spirit dreams and actual conversations. All other names – apart from the koala named David, whose story I have already told in 'The Mirror of the Fatal Shore' – have been changed. "Aldous" may bear a certain resemblance to the novelist and intellectual Aldous Huxley, but it would be folly to identify the one with the other. As far as "Humbert J Brockenhurst" goes, there is no noted figure in the annals of Theosophy with that name, to the best of my knowledge: while I assure my readers that "Humbert" is indeed based on a real person, the true name of this worthy individual will remain my secret.

The same, of course, goes for the people in Part Two. Again, secrecy must prevail.

Except that "Rollo Rodney" is largely fictional.

As a non-poetry reader, "Dorothea"'s experience of bird talk and her recounting of it are unlikely to have been influenced by Attar's great poem *The Conference of the Birds* (or *The Bird-Parliament*): there's scant resemblance, anyway.

And a few details in conversations and narration have been altered: very few, however, and only where deemed necessary.

Have I said that I once met John Cage? It was 1972 or '73, in the Swiss Cottage Hotel. I was curious, so I arranged to meet him. I'd asked my friend Sydney Carter, songwriter, singer and poet, to come with me, but Sydney felt he didn't know Cage's work well enough. In the event, a couple of other poet/musician friends accompanied me, and staged an impromptu event for Cage in the hotel foyer. I was embarrassed: it seemed...*too much.*

Cage was very camp and quite bitchy. I don't know how else to say it. He told stories about long term friends and artistic allies like Mark Tobey and Morton Feldman that seemed quite unkind, as if he needed to feel superior to them in some way. I certainly wasn't disturbed by Cage's campness, merely naively surprised. I was concerned by the bitchiness, however. I didn't take to him. Ah well.

Alan Watts' criticism of Cage, which I've alluded to, occurs in his booklet *Beat Zen Square Zen and Zen* (SF: City Lights Books, 1959).

Echoes and snippets of koala wisdom appear in the writings of diverse thinkers, including Simone Weil, Rudolf Arnheim and James J Gibson. Whether this is sheer coincidence or something of a deeper nature, I really can't say. Needless to say, all these thinkers go wrong at some point or other.

More of the back story of 'Beyond the Mirror of the Fatal Shore' can be found in the aforementioned piece 'The Mirror of the Fatal Shore', included in my collection *Towards a Menagerie* (Tucson: Chax Press, 2019).

'Beyond the Mirror of the Fatal Shore' was written down in 2018.

Spoiler Alert:

Despite what the first pages may suggest, this is most definitely *not* a children's tale.

Messages for Dominic

I can't imagine that Robert Lax wouldn't have mentioned his friend Ad Reinhardt, another "right artist".

Surely Reinhardt, for all his "art-as-art" dogma, absolutely goes beyond aesthetic criteria – composition, harmony, decoration, beauty, ocular pleasure.... His art is irritating, frustrating... and yet ultimately as overwhelmingly transcendent – in the larger sense of *going beyond* – as Barnett Newman's, in its own utterly unique way.

Attention is at the heart of Reinhardt's painting, as it is with Lax's writing. I remember the first time I saw some of R's "all-black" paintings. 1968? Something like that. I didn't have a clue. I walked past them and thought that those few people standing in front of them and looking, looking, were fools. I was the fool. You didn't see anything if you didn't stand there and look and look.

Ad Reinhardt's late paintings are mysterious, exasperating, infinitely complex and at the same time devastatingly simple. Beginning in 1960 he painted a long series of "black" paintings of a single format (square, large but not immense); the paintings appear to be simply black monochromes, without any apparent modulation over the entire area of the painting (and hence without formal/spatial relations). In fact, the paintings were done in extremely dark tones that possess only very subtle differences yet are derived from distinct colours; these tones were used to paint nine equal squares which link up (or intersect) in such a way as to form a Greek cross. This single design was repeated by Reinhardt for each painting in the series – so that the paintings differ in only infinitesimal ways.

The experience of seeing a Reinhardt painting is unlike that of any other artist's work: it requires long and intense scrutiny before details of the cross-shape begin to emerge, but as soon as they do they disappear again into the black monochrome field, and the process of this appearing and disappearing, and the degree of attention required to reveal and hold on to the details (never strong enough to hold them for long), is strangely awe-inspiring – there is a powerful sense of "mystery" involved, even if one knows how the painting is composed and why it "behaves" as it does – and is also exasperating. Photographs are useless.

It was an extreme point, or position: so extreme that he referred to his paintings as "the end of art". The poet Susan Howe commented that if this is represented as silence, it is a silence full of messages. The "simplicity" of his paintings, she said, more precisely, is "alive with messages". By which one means? I'd say: the paradoxical co-incidence of visibility and invisibility, image and imagelessness, form and formlessness, colour and colourlessness, relation and non-relation: and all of what *that* can mean to someone. But the experience of the painting is what one always comes back to.

Robert Lax did talk to me about Reinhardt when I visited him. (Yes, I did visit him... in 1973 first, and a couple of times later. Many people did.) But I think I'd already become interested in A R by then.

The great negator, I think Reinhardt called himself, no, no, *demurrer*, in a time of great enthusiasms. And I remember someone wrote an essay in one of the art journals, contrasting him with Andy Warhol, that great enthusiast.

My sympathies lie with Reinhardt.

......

I can't say whether or not Dom really knew Lax or not, or, for that matter, the Themersons; but what he says of them rings true. (Yes. I knew the Themersons, too; in fact they published one of my first books.)

....

I've utilised fragments from a couple of writings of my mine in working up this piece and these notes: a review of Michael N McGregor's *Pure Act: The Uncommon Life of Robert Lax* (Fordham UP, 2015), which appeared in the online journal *Stride* in 2016, and from 'Notes Written at a Night Window: On Ad Reinhardt', which appeared in my book *Art and Disclosure: Seven Essays* (Stride Publications, 1998).

If you're going to plagiarise – steal – scavenge from – anyone, it might as well be yourself.

I realise I could be accused of blowing my own trumpet here. But then, as the saying goes, who else is going to?

I'm also briefly quoting from Susan Howe's essay 'The End of Art', which Nicholas Zurbrugg and I included in *The ABCs of Robert Lax* (Stride Publications, 1999).

Mention of *Stride* and Stride Publications gives me the opportunity to thank the editor/publisher, Rupert Loydell, for many years of support and friendship.

Lax's '21 pages' appeared as a book, *21 pages / 21 seiten*, with a German translation by Alfred Kuoni, from pendo verlag in 1984. It was reprinted in its entirety in *The Alchemist's Mind: a book of narrative prose by poets*, which I edited for Reality Street in 2012.

......

The brief quotation from Emmanuel Swedenborg is from his *Heaven and Hell*, tr George F Dole, Swedenborg Foundation, (2002) 2012.

The Simone Weil quotation (from a letter to the poet Joë Bousquet) is taken from Jacques Cabaud, *Simone Weil: A Fellowship in Love*, Channel Press, 1964.

......

Dom's first dream of Iredell is reminiscent of an old cartoon which shows an encounter between a fashionable-looking Victorian lady and equally fashionable-looking gentleman, both equipped with banjos while out on a stroll; one asks the other for a note on their instrument so they can tune up. I found this in a banjo instruction manual by Pete Seeger (*How to Play the 5-string Banjo*, Homespun Music Instruction, 1961), where it's ascribed to G Du Maurier – presumably George du Maurier, cartoonist for *Punch* and the author of *Peter Ibbetson*. I can't imagine Iredell would ever have seen it.

......

The singer Nico was supposed to have said that during the time she was a heroin addict she mainly lived on custard, which she described as being scarcely like food at all. But of course it is. You may think that this text is scarcely a story at all: yet it is. Of course it is.

......

I wrote this piece in 2019.

I would like to thank my (late) wife, Dodo, Marcia Kelly (Robert Lax Literary Trust), and Jasia Reichardt (Themerson Archive), for feedback... advice... encouragement.

True Points

An earlier version of this piece appeared in *The Alchemist's Mind: a book of narrative prose by poets*, which I edited for Reality Street (2012).

An even earlier version was included in my chapbook *True Points: Eight Prose Texts 1981-1987* (Spectacular Diseases Press, 1992). Those were the heady days when small independent publishers and journals seemed to vie with each other for... well, *heady* names. It was a very fine, adventurous press, no matter what.

I haven't any idea where the brief quotation from the philosopher F E Sparshott comes from, although I seem to recall it was an essay on aesthetics.

The quotation about the ways in which divine Being "is revealed in every being and yet always hidden in them" is taken from Ernesto Grassi's fascinating (if largely misguided) book *Heidegger and the Question of Renaissance Humanism: Four Studies* (SUNY at Binghampton, 1983).

I seem to have been circling around many of the same themes, sources etc for a very long time, even if I've approached them in different ways and with different outcomes: either an admirable single-mindedness or a woeful lack of curiosity: hopefully the former.

The King's Three Bodies

Even though I'm a third generation Australian who only left Australia for England at the age of 21, my grasp of Aussie slang isn't what it might be. I've relied fairly heavily on *Stunned Mullets & Two-Pot Screamers*, compiled by G A Wilkes (5th ed., OUP, 2008). I suspect much of this can be guessed at, although it may help to explain that "boong" is a disrespectful term for an Aboriginal Australian, and a "two-pot screamer" is someone who drinks too much (though Aussie friend Ken White suggests it's more a question of someone who can't hold their liquor and acts foolishly accordingly). "Cobber" is apparently scarcely used any more, but I like it. "Donald": rhyming slang.

Please note: I use "indigenous" with a small "i". I also apologise to those who prefer "First Nation people" (or variants) to "Aboriginal Australians".

Sixpence to Spend is a children's book by Ida Rentoul Outhwaite, published in 1935. As far as I can make out, it's never been republished, and is indeed quite rare. Publishers? Any interest?

I've been somewhat unfair in suggesting that the Lutheran Church would inflict the sort of "counselling" indicated in this story on one of their pastors: nothing in my own experience of Lutheranism accords with this, nor the idea that they'd be "removed" to a university chaplaincy: so, apologies! Also, please don't "identify" "Pastor Bob" or "Pastor Jasna" (or indeed any of the characters): this would be a mistaken course, as my story *is* a work of fiction.

"Who said that history is a nightmare we're trying to wake up from?" Paraphrasing the character Stephen Daedalus, in James Joyce's *Ulysses* (1922).

"Language is the Throne of the Other": the once fashionable (and probably in some circles still fashionable) French psychoanalyst and psychoanalytical theorist Jacques Lacan.

I have to admit that I have grave doubts about Ed the Koala being the author of the Ern Malley poems (*if* that indeed is what is really implied). I corresponded with Harold Stewart, who was as it were one half of "Ern Malley", in the early 1970s. The English Buddhist Marco Pallis put me in touch with him because I was interested in Shin Buddhism and Harold was a long-time follower of Shin. I can honestly say that Harold never even hinted that the Malley poems (*The Darkening Ecliptic*) were based on the writings of a koala, nor that they had been written by anyone else than himself and his friend James McAuley. Significantly, Michael Heyward's book *The Ern Malley Affair* (QUP, 1993) doesn't mention Ed at all.

"Although our knowledge of our soul is not complete, what we do know of it through consciousness or inner sensation is enough to demonstrate its immortality, spirituality, freedom, and several other attributes we need to know." Nicolas Malebranche, 'The Search After Truth' (*Philosophical Selections*, ed Steven Nadler, Indianapolis / Cambridge: Hackett Publishing, 1992; tr by Thomas M Lennon and Paul J Olscamp). King Archie was more widely read than some might have thought!

Did Sir Laurie confuse "inflammable" with the concept of "infallible"? I don't believe so.

A Koala Rhapsody

First published as a limited edition broadsheet from Kater Murr's Press (Athens, Greece) in 2021. God bless the Cat.

About the Author

David Miller was born in Melbourne, Australia, but has lived in the UK for many years. His recent publications include *Spiritual Letters (Series 1-5)* (Chax Press, 2011), *Reassembling Still: Collected Poems* (Shearsman Books, 2014), *Spiritual Letters* (Contraband Books, 2017 / Spuyten Duyvil, 2022), *Towards a Menagerie* (Chax Press, 2019), *Matrix I & II* (Guillemot Press, 2020), *Some Other Days and Nights* (above/ground press, 2021), *Afterword* (Shearsman Books, 2022), *circle square triangle* (Spuyten Duyvil, 2022), *An Envelope for Silence* (above/ground press, 2022) and *Some Other Shadows* (Knives Forks and Spoons Press, 2022). He is also a painter and a musician.

About CHAX

Chax Press has always sought to bring a sense of expanded possibility to the book, acted out in content, design, typography, materials, and structures. We began in 1984 and have published some 250 books, including artists' books, fine press books, hybrid letterpress-digital books, chapbooks, trade paperback books, and casebound or boxed publications. In 2021 the Chax Press director received the Lord Nose Award (named in honor of the legendary Jonathan Williams of The Jargon Society), conferred by the Community of Literary Magazines and Presses (CLMP), for lifetime achievement in literary publishing.

Chax is a nonprofit 501(c)(3) organization which depends on suppport from various government & private funders, and, primarly, from individual donors and readers. Please join our mission by supporting Chax. You will find us online at https://chax.org, and you can email us at chaxpress@chax.org.

Correspondence to the press should be sent to Chax Press / 1517 N Wilmot Rd no. 264 / Tucson AZ 85712 / USA

The font used in this book is Adobe Caslon
Book & Cover Design by Charles Alexander
Cover art by David Miller: *Dodo's* (ink painting)
Printer & Binder: KC Book Manufacturing